# Atlantic
# Hijack

## By Sam Grant

Published by Sam Grant

Publishing partner: Paragon Publishing, Rothersthorpe
© Sam Grant 2014

ISBN 978-1-78222-291-0

Book design, layout and production management by Into Print
www.intoprint.net
+44 (0)1604 832149

Printed and bound in UK and USA by Lightning Source

# Ocean Melody Prepares for Departure

Winter sun glinted on the nearby crane shut down for the day. A rope sling moved to and fro, dangling in the breeze, from the cargo hook, like food remnant in the mouth of a tall herbivore fallen asleep in the midst of eating. Six years had passed, since Motor Vessel Albany Princess was taken over by terrorists. Reuters reported it as a "disruption" on cargo liner Albany Princess voyaging toward South America—played down, because I suspect the government wanted to avoid conflict with Argentina over The Falklands.

Six years on from November, 1962 now aboard the cargo liner Ocean Melody I was preparing for a repeat of the same voyage with the responsibilities of Second Mate. A circle of movement aboard other ships, bringing me back to the trade route from Liverpool to The Cape Verde islands for bunkering, followed by a stop at Montevideo, and finally unloading the bulk of the cargo at Buenos Aires. Recollections returned of Albany Princess in Liverpool then.

How at the end of the day Tom the senior apprentice and myself played four a side football in a dockside warehouse. The Second and Third Mate on our team against the Second, Fourth, Fifth and Sixth engineers. We practised when possible, because the ship got together a team to play against other ship's docked in Buenos Aires. In the years after my apprenticeship I served on a tanker fetching oil from Nigeria for Thames Haven, then loading oil in the Middle East for Japan. An ore carrier that went to Liberia, Sweden, Norway, Nova Scotia and Lima, Peru, for iron ore, and a tanker contracted for a year running from Venezuela to New York carrying boiler oil. Lima, Peru being the nearest

I got to Argentina, albeit on the west and not east coast of South America. Travelling the same route again on Ocean Melody, but now as Second Mate. It was four fifteen and only the deck cargo remained to be secured. Dave Green, the Mate allowed me to finish early, to check that necessary charts were ready. 'I'll see to this Mike, you can cut off now,' he said. Normally my cargo watching didn't finish until the last stevedore was at the foot of the gangway. Now we were near to sailing. No departure time mentioned, but ship's do not earn their keep in port. With cargo loading completed the company would want us on our way. High tide not far off meant a good depth of water in the buoyed channel leading out of port. This reminiscing about my experiences from the past was interrupted by the voice of the Second Steward. His white coat and gold buttons standing out against the dirt on the green lifeboat cover as he walked by. In his mid-twenties about my age.

'Just heard Mr Green telling the stevedore manager we're sailing at seven and he wants the deck cargo fully secured. Thought you'd like to know,' he said, slowing on his way to the next companionway. A tray of cups and saucers embossed with the company's red and white pennant, cradled in hand and fore arm.

'Thanks Pete. Good of you to update me on classified information,' I replied jokingly. He smiled back. We first met when I was Third Mate on an ore carrier and Peter a saloon steward. Both of us since gaining seniority. Dave Green would more than likely have gotten around to telling me about sailing. Safe stowage being priority over all else, at present. Peter continued up the next companionway. A steady clatter of the stevedores feet on the aluminium gangway accompanied me leaving the boat deck. In my cabin I removed my boiler suit, then showered and put on a uniform jacket and trousers before making for the Chart Room.

Apart from being officer of the watch on the twelve to four at sea there was the responsibility of plotting the great circle course required to navigate the ship by the shortest route to South America. Star Azimuths (the arc altitude of stars, and planets above the horizon) then taken by sextant on the twelve to four watch to get a "fix" on the ship's position, in the pre-dawn. Stars and horizon both visible until the sun, duster like wipes the night sky away. I followed the Radio Officer, John Coates down the companionway from the bridge to the main accommodation deck before sitting opposite him in the dining saloon. A long table, which seated those of us with fewer than three seniority bands on our arms. We were followed by Captain Bellamy and Dave Green, who entered the saloon just as we sat down

'I'm not having anyone in the saloon in tee shirt or work clothes Mr Green. You can pass the message on to everyone who dines in this saloon. And you as well Mr Peters,' said Captain Bellamy, momentarily raising his hand to catch my attention as he stepped into the saloon. His fog horn voice penetrating down the corridor, I sensed, without a need for either of us to transmit the order. I was innocently inspecting the menu held out by the Steward, before getting hauled into the conversation. Nodding agreement in a way that I hoped looked approving. Around the coast relief crews dressed as they pleased. With various office and maintenance contractors on board it became difficult to spot actual ship's officers in the dining saloon. Captain Bellamy was of the old school. War service defined by ribbons on his uniform. None of us more youthful officers had seen action. My pre-sea training of parades and inspections gave understanding about uniform and discipline. I felt for the engineers who mainly came from a civilian environment. Perhaps giving up wearing uniform when in the sixth form at school. The saloon filled up with officers including the two ship's apprentices.

Everyone I noted was in uniform. Dave Green, looked across and smiled in acknowledgement that the message appeared to have reached all concerned without any assistance from us. A tug's whistle sounded as I left the saloon. That hoarse strangulated whistle not making full pitch. Not an impatient and in a hurry sort of whistle more a—"look I'm here now, when you're ready to leave,"—kind of toot. Nevertheless it came from the stern and that was my station for leaving port. Within ten minutes I was back into my boiler suit, having grabbed a torch and gloves before making for the after deck. 'The pilot's aboard Second Mate,' the Bosun called out as I arrived. 'Made the Bridge by now—the speed of them feet up the gangway,' he continued. Smoke from the tug's tall funnel, blew across leaving a foul taste in my mouth. The intercom buzzed not long afterwards.

'Tell the Bosun he can hoist up the gangway,' said Captain Bellamy speaking from inside the wheel house The Bosun over hearing the order, raised his hand in acknowledgement taking the deck boy and an AB (Able-bodied seaman) with him to the gangway. I heard the Captain speaking to the pilot in the background but couldn't make anything out before he was back and said, 'You there Second?' 'Yes' 'Has the tug got the tow wire?' It was wrapped around the bits, but lying slack from the towing band on the tug. 'Yes, it's secured on board,' I replied. 'Good, good,' said Captain Bellamy. 'You can let go. Let me know when all lines are clear of the water.' Flood lights from the mast head flooded the deck, but the quayside was dark. I shone my torch across. Out of the gloom a voice came back—'Slacken your lines Second Mate. We're ready when you are.' Two sailors were to hand assisted by the deck apprentice. 'You can release that rope,' I said and pointed at the bitts near to the winch. By the time the Bosun returned water was trickling from coils of rope winched aboard by number five hold with the tug tightening on the tow wire. I walked to the stern rail to check on progress. The nearby winch was running at full speed with two rope turns round the drum. The final rope was lifted clear of the water and propeller. 'Stern to bridge. All ropes clear,' I said standing about three inches back from the perforated metal voice box beneath the speaker. Dick Rawlins—the Third Mate replied. 'Message received, all ropes clear on afterdeck. Captain and pilot notified.' And moments later the message back from Dick, 'Over and out.' 'Not out, the intercoms still open Third,' I said, 'This isn't ship to shore radio.' 'You know what I mean,' he said and was gone. I caught Captain Bellamy's deep voice in the background calling him. Timber and sawdust left from securing cargo littered the deck area. Tarpaulins like unmade beds were crumpled across hatches. A twang came from the towing wire tensed by the tug's grip, 'Get away from that tow rope.' An eighteen year old, who as an EDH (Efficient Deck Hand), should have known better was standing by the tug's wire. The thrust from the propeller foamed the water as it pulled at the ship's stern. Wire crunched on the bits from the tension. I was annoyed with myself for shouting aggressively, yet needed to get him away from danger. Tug hawsers can snap in whip like fashion, cutting through limbs and bodies. Captain Bellamy's intercom voice broke through the rapid beat of the tug's engine. 'How many boats lengths are we away from the dock wall, now, Second?' he asked.

This Captain measured in what he called boat lengths of twenty feet. Luckily Dave Green told me about this idiosyncrasy when I boarded. It was a good idea because it made you count across the water in a measured way. The human eye tended to underestimate when informing the brain of number approximation. The Captain could guess the distance from the bridge, but I was able to look along the five hundred foot length of Ocean Melody, viewing bow and stern. The bow now farthest from the dock wall. 'Ten boat lengths at the stern and fifteen for the bow,' I replied. 'Nothing like enough yet pilot,' the Captain's voice fading as he moved away from the mouthpiece, before returning 'Let me know at twenty boat's length for the stern, got that Second?' 'The tug's getting a grip, it should be soon,' I replied. The ship needed manoeuvring into the dock basin's open water before the tugs turned the bow seawards. The good ship handling abilities of both pilot and Captain required to get the timing right with ships berthed nearby. The ship moved outwards and forward. I kept Captain Bellamy informed about our distance from the dock walls. The pilot then neatly swung the ship around assisted by the bow and stern tugs. Once clear of the docks my deck duty came to an end, but for the Bosun work was only just beginning, as sailors gathered on the after deck. His distinctive call of—'The next song will be a dance me lads, to get these hatches secured.' One of several expressions used by him to induce work enthusiasm in the crew, but also perhaps in the belief that he possessed especial comic ability.

It was eight thirty when I sat down in my cabin situated on the second deck up from the main deck. A few hours respite before going on watch at midnight. I drew the curtains across the porthole, reached toward the shelf above the day bed and extracted an old journal, after lifting clear a mahogany band positioned along the middle to prevent books jumping out at sea. I opened the roughly scribbled A4 hard backed book, which served then, in 1962, as a practice log. There in the centre was a photo of Albany Princess viewed from the end of Dock Sud, Buenos Aires. Streaks of rust on the black painted hull, but the name lettering clear, freshly painted by us, that's Tom and me while alongside in Montevideo. The rise of the bow above the dock emphasised by the steep angle of the mooring ropes. Six or more flat-bed lorries double parked by its side. Crates already strapped on to some. Others lowered by the ship's derricks from above. Jane, having worked her passage from the UK asked me to take a photo. I took two for good measure. They both came out and I glued the spare one inside the book. That photo reminded me of how we first met, but also at that time the relief I felt that Jane was safe back on board with her mother and Christina.

# Chapter 1

# Aboard Motor Vessel Albany Princess
# September 1962

I was one of two apprentices arriving at the Port of Liverpool after a three week voyage or "trip" as they are known. I was on my second trip as apprentice with a better idea about what is expected going into port. The high level of finesse, for example, required aboard the bridge of a cargo liner. Both anchoring and docking I found exciting. The gimballed magnetic compass face danced about in front of the wheel, but it was the clicking Giro compass, housed at the side in a blue metal box, which was for steering by. It was rarely more than a degree out from true north. I remember that time being wheelman on the four to eight watch on the approach to the Liverpool anchorage. The Mate left the bridge to attend to anchoring from the f'oc'sl'e while Captain Smith took charge of ship management. He walked to the port side of the bridge several times looking down to check the ship's speed through the water with the engine at stop. He called back to the Third Mate in the wheelhouse. '—Dead Slow Astern.' A low level rumble from the engine and seconds later with battery powered megaphone in hand he blasted from the bridge '—Let go the starboard anchor Mr Mate. The Mate responded by criss-crossing his hands above his head. The red rust visible on deck before we heard the noise of the anchor wrenching the cable from the quiet of the locker. '—Stop engines,' '—Stop engines,' Captain repeated the Third Mate. The telegraph buzzed as he moved it to stop. Intermittent clunks from the cable interrupted the quiet, as the ship gripped on the anchor. My observational role was interrupted by a shriek of boiler steam from the funnel and a rapid drum roll of cable from the port anchor release. The evening darkened as fog moved in to wrap itself around the ship. 'Go down on deck lad and get masthead lights switched on. See what Mate wants,' said Captain Smith as he came back into the wheelhouse. I stepped down from the raised wooden plinth my wheelman duty finished. The painted canvas hand rail made slippery from the fog decided me against a customary hand slide to the mid-section of the companionways, on the way down but jumped midway from the final stairway on to the after deck. I entered the mast house between four and five holds turning the switches to light the overhead mast spotlights. Other than the glow above they made little impression on the deck. A run back to the stairway. A short walk along the mid-accommodation deck and down to the foredeck to switch on the mast lights between two and three holds. The Mate spotted me about to enter the foremost masthead locker. He was under six foot with a ruddy complexion—head of white wavy hair now covered with a black commando style woollen hat. The three gold arm bands of rank were clearly visible. He wore his uniform jacket over a spotless white boiler suit. He leant forward from the f 'o'c'sl'e railing above, hands cupped over mouth to make himself heard. 'We won't be going anywhere in a hurry son, while the fog lasts. Have your meal and take the seven to eight lookout up here.' 'Right sir,' I said, while releasing the handle to open the masthead door.

Motor Vessel Albany Princess, an 8,000 ton cargo liner was returning from Uruguay and Argentina fully loaded with fifty bales of wool on deck. Shifting boards in one, two and three lower holds held together mounds of grain. Higher quality bagged grain stacked with bales of wool and cotton in the 'tween decks. Sorghum, soya, linseed and sunflower seed, some bagged some not. Tinned apples, pears, in tins the size of buckets, corned beef, tongue, bagged hooves and bones. The lower hold of number five full of onions, complete with chirping crickets !!

# Chapter 2

# Tom and Mike

At 8,000 tons Albany Princess was fairly typical of a general cargo ship of the nineteen sixties. Five cargo holds, three masts, derricks, prominent funnel above the cabin space, five piston engine, three generators, a crew of fifty four and two deck apprentices. In this instance, Tom Blake and myself, Mike Peters. In a world of being thrown together for months on end you needed to get on as apprentices. Tom at nineteen was eighteen months older and confident in his position as senior apprentice. Blond spiky hair whitened by the sun, bulkier than me, but not as tall. Our cabins small, but containing a wash stand, wardrobe, bunk with drawers, and a settee called a day bed. Each cabin had a porthole opening on to the deck outside. Also a Formica desk, which Tom was sitting at, when I returned from switching on the mast head lights. Sleeves rolled up, tie and uniform jacket, flung on the day bed behind. The cabins being next door meant we invariably met up. I grabbed the ledge above Tom's cabin door, attempting chin ups, but not keeping my legs totally clear of his desk. On reflection my younger self must have been especially irritating at times.

'Do you have to Mike?' he said. I lowered myself down and sat on the floral patterned day bed. 'I've just passed the Third Engineer's cabin. That silver framed photo he has on his desk. I've never seen that before. He's got a very young wife.' 'That's not his wife Mike—' he said, glancing at me like a teacher might a student in need of extra tuition. Simplifying information from Tom's lofty heights was happening less often—than when I first joined as Junior Apprentice. 'It's his eldest daughter. He puts that framed photo on the cabin desk, when we reach the UK. A sort of ritual. Could be to remind himself he's married, with a stunner of a daughter.' 'She's not bad looking,' I said, feigning indifference. 'Not bad looking. Is there something wrong with your sight? She's a honey. The Third says she goes to the Electric Dance Hall on Saturday, She's a nurse, apparently.' 'You told him you might be going to the Electric Hall?' 'No, he just said, that the picture was taken when she was eighteen and now she's twenty two and goes to dances at the Electric Hall. He just happened to mention it. What odds are there of her being there and you meeting her?' 'That's if we dock before Saturday,' I said, 'anyway.' '—Mike if we sign off early, you're still up for a night ashore, before you go on leave aren't you?' he said turning his chair to face me.

I remembered that there was mention of this earlier. Tom took his main leave in Argentina, where his family lived and remained on board while the ship was discharging in the UK. 'That was the bet,' said Tom, that if we docked early you'd catch the train on Sunday. Tom looked hard at me to ensure he got the answer he wanted. 'Okay, okay,' I said. 'There's a disco dance there on Saturday. It's got a resident group and will be packed with talent. The girls are allowed in free, which means there's a good selection.' Tom spoke as if the girls were provided like some in house movie. I had agreed that I would stay and go ashore, if we docked before the weekend.

Larger cargo liners with twin propellers carrying mail and passengers were predictable—aiming to arrive for berthing on a specific day and tide. Motor cargo ships, with one propeller like ours, less easy to predict, but Tom bet the Third Mate two hundred pesos, left over from Buenos Aires, about making port before Saturday. The bet with me, that if we docked on Friday I'd stay over to go ashore—Saturday. Tom was less likely to win with the fog, but knowing his luck he might.

He was taking the opportunity to catch up on course work. 'Why does the Mate have to be so damned helpful?

13

He's just told me he'll post it when he goes on leave,' said Tom, turning the page on the stapled course work chapter. On leaving Buenos Aires Tom asked the Mate if he could go on day work. I remembered this. We were cleaning the brasses in the wheelhouse. 'I really need time to catch up, I'm not far off taking study leave for the Second Mate's Certificate, Chief. Day work would allow time in the evenings for extra study, if that's all right?' The Mate, agreed, but said he expected results. Day Work meant reporting to the Bosun and working through until five with a midday meal break, interspersed with ten minute morning and afternoon coffee breaks. The breaks were called 'Smoko's'. The Mate's offer to post two months completed course work was a subtle way of ensuring Tom kept his side of the bargain. Not all First Mates were as accommodating as Mr Thompson. Some expected you to be on watch keeping duties and put in time chipping, scraping, painting, holy stoning decks and cleaning brasses during the day. Not all at the same time. Although probably that's what they might have liked. Then too exhausted for much studying, in the evening.

'The Mate's just said we're unlikely to go in before the fog lifts,' I mentioned to Tom. 'I've got to take the seven to eight f'o'c'sl'e watch. Bit of luck for you Tom this fog. The delay I mean.' 'I'd have finished this. Bit of pressure, that's all. Thrive under a bit of pressure, you know me Mike.' That was it I did, but decided not to contradict him on this point. I retreated to my cabin. After showering I changed into white shirt, black tie, doeskin jacket and trousers for the evening meal. Gold flashes on the jacket lapels, indicated deck apprentice—not the gold arm band denoting officer rank. I needed to get a shift on to be on watch by seven. It was my first time as lookout on the f'o'c'sl'e at anchor in fog.

Fred the able-bodied sailor I was taking over from, demonstrated the bell ringing procedure and left me to it. The heavy brass bell, sounded ominously on its own accord, when the ship pitched in heavy seas. It now required sounding eleven or twelve times, every five minutes, to warn ships that we were at anchor.

There was the drip, drip of condensing fog falling from the foremast and alarmingly close whistle blasts from nearby shipping. I counted five minutes, before sounding the bell to start with, before resorting to checking my wrist watch. When there were no ships whistles, it went quiet, save for waves eerily slapping, the ship's side. The ship responding to wind and tidal flow, caused occasional crunches from the starboard anchor cable. The forward part of the green tarpaulin on number one hatch was visible, but not much else. The wheelhouse windows were enveloped in fog, but light from the lower accommodation windows was visible.

At 1955 hours the eight to twelve watchman took over. 'Get some shut eye, son. This may clear overnight. Just take a strong offshore breeze and you'll see this'll be gone,' were the sailor's parting words. I was happy to end that watch and stroll back along the damp red deck—to step into brightly lit corridors—reassured by the pulsating clatter from one of the three ship's generators.

# Chapter 3

# At Anchor

I remember the quarter to four call being early, but the crew were keyed up for signing off and going on leave. The previous twelve to four watch saw it as important to get me on watch five minutes early. Now, no longer assessed for making it to the bridge on time. My being awake not in doubt—the call of 'Open your eyes,' to see for certain that I was awake and not lost in a dream, no longer seen necessary as when on my first trip. That's what hits you though, the cold. It was colder than it needed to be, since I preferred having the port hole open and the hot air blower closed. I didn't like waking with a dry mouth and throat. The donkey jacket, roll neck pullover, jeans, heavy socks, and Doc Martens, meant dressing absorbed more time, than just the shirt, shorts and flip flops, we wore in the Tropics. A tingling tremor ran up my spine, and across my back I recall. I attributed this to the cold, but perhaps, now in retrospect a subconscious fore-warning of what lay in the months ahead.

When called again by the watch I was dressed with the cabin door open. 'Your mate could do with some training from you. He's no easy one to wake,' said the sailor standing in the open door space. 'Really,' I said with an element of surprise in my voice. 'Perhaps it's just as well he's on day work.' 'Aye, it is that. You'll be taking over from Jack on the Monkey Island, then, shortly.' 'Yep,' I replied. Satisfied I was awake he left.

Sleep plays tricks and deckhands discovered that a sensible conversation with Tom with eyes wide open, did not necessarily mean he was really awake. Demands like lift your arm to show me or repeated questioning of 'Are you really awake,' to the point of annoyance was needed to ensure he was fully out of deep sleep. That the Mate allowed Tom to go on day work homeward bound, was probably a relief for this earlier watch.

The door leading to the mid-deck was like a porthole in the outer housing. Raised above deck level, to help prevent storm water entering the accommodation. Not lifting your foot meant kicking the raised metal lip—not an unusual occurrence for me, when about to go on watch in the middle of the night. As I stepped outside the sight of the fog around the companionway, together with the rush of cold air to the lungs, sharpened my wakefulness.

I felt the metal treads through my shoes going up the companionway, hands slipping on moisture laden handrails. Jack already at the top of the companionway, leading to the Monkey Island called 'Good on you cobber,' before I was half way up. Jack a man of few words didn't stop to chat.

While at anchor the lookout assisted the officer of the watch, as required, but was still expected to report passing ships. The direction of ships whistles were very difficult to pinpoint in fog, but a noticeable increase in loudness needed instantly report-ing—via the voice pipe. The officer of the watch would increase the whistle frequency of two short followed by one long blasts dramatically, from the minimum interval of once every two minutes, to signal our being at anchor. The literal code transla-tion being—"You are standing into danger."

The Mate called up from the bridge just below. 'You can come down from there and make some coffee son. Then take a Decca bearing. Good practice for you.' Chief Officer Bert Thompson, known as The Mate, wore glasses. He returned to sea after running an ironmongers store in Cardiff whose business dried up. He returned to sea as First Mate. The years spent being agreeable to customers, rather than managing gangs of sailors probably enriched his personality, if not his bank account.

# Previous Encounter with River Bank Leads to Dry Docking

Albany Princess was a premier ship for carrying general cargo from the UK to Argentina. Loading and securing cargo a complex task, making use of cranes, ship's derricks and gangs of stevedores. Containers in an experimental stage outward bound. Small garage size ones used to secure boxed whisky, brandy, gin and Drambuie. Then with wires shackled to metal rings on top. They were lifted and lowered into the holds.

A traditional ship's wheel occupied the centre spot in the wheelhouse with a Tele-motor system. A turn of the wheel hydraulically pushed oil through sealed pipes which operated the steering engines next to the rudder. There was a separate automatic pilot mechanism for switching on, when away from the coast. Incorporated within this a push button electronic steering mechanism, independent of the hydraulic ship's wheel. Wheelman generally preferred the feel of the "real" ship's wheel, but needed competency with both methods of steering. A Decca radar, echo Sounder and engine telegraphs at both ends next to the sliding doors. When standing on the bridge an invisible man effect created. The telegraph handle appearing to move by itself when altered from the handle within the wheelhouse.

A logline ran out from the portside of the bridge attached to a spinner recording sea miles travelled on a dial. An expanse of windows defined the thirty plus foot wheelhouse on top of the mid-ships accommodation. The wheelhouse gave eyes and ears to the navigator in present time, that's when without fog. The chart room leading off from the wheelhouse recorded progress and in particular position. Charts were housed beneath the desk and a chronometer set in gimbals with a glass viewing panel. The chronometer might register a very slight gain or loss. This being constant enabling the correction to be applied for accurate Greenwich Mean Time, essential for longitudinal position finding, day and night. Radio signals bleeping GMT were available for spot checks.

I was in the chart room pencilling in signals from the Decca Navigator when Sparks entered from the accommodation wearing a uniform jacket over striped pyjamas. A dress statement to advertise sleep rudely interrupted by having to man the radio. 'We're safe at last with a top man in charge,' he said. I ignored him. A coastal yachtsman, he joined bridge navigators in the tropics attempting to calculate the Day's Run. To the merriment of the Second Mate, one of his practice calculations positioned Albany Princess in the middle of the Sahara Desert.

Making coffee, tidying the wheelhouse, interspersed with taking Decca radio bearings was my lot as junior apprentice. He passed into the wheelhouse holding a message for the Mate. 'Thanks Sparks,' I heard the Mate say, before reading it out. '0600 hours: Cutter progressing. Pilot's arrival, thirty minutes, Max. Regards, Pilot Station.' 'The fog must be lifting around the coast,' said the Mate. 'I've been chatting with a radio officer leaving port on a BP tanker. There's no fog a mile out. It's sweeping away, so he says.' 'No time to waste, then,' said the Mate, the phone buzzing as he called the engine room. 'Fog's lifting, we'll be needing power in twenty minutes, Third,' he said, 'Let the Chief know we're going in shortly.' Sparks came back through to return to his radio and keyboard, followed by the Mate. 'I'll give the Old Man ten minutes more shut eye. Dig out the watch son, they need to get the pilot ladder ready. You can take a coffee break, but be on the wheel before the pilot boards.'

I slid the door open on to the bridge deck from the wheel-house. The brass treads on the companionways were slippery on my way down to the crew's accommodation. The décor was dark green and the deck tiles a mottled blue and red, contrasting with the officer's ivory and beige. The Seaman's Mess Room comprised six light green Formica topped tables and those chrome chairs which curled and appear to be unsupported, but had tubes of toughened steel. A print of the Queen trooping the colour above the serving hatch led from the galley and a print of Constable's Haywain on the inner bulkhead (wall).

I made up the third member, of the deck watch—Dave and George the other two. They were sitting opposite each other playing cards in the centre of the Mess Room. Dave was in jeans and pullover, George in jeans and tee shirt. A tattooed heart with an arrow and Rosie intertwined on his arm. 'We're going in, in half an hour,' I said. 'The Chief wants the pilot ladder made ready.'—Dave looked at George—'How's that to be? With fog out there.' George, placed his cards face down on the table went to a porthole and pulled the curtain back. 'Could be right, it's nowhere like as thick outside.'

George on the first trip told me off for swearing. 'I can swear, but you can't. The crowd,' (that's the crew), 'will not respect you. They won't see you as more skilled or able than them, even if it's an act.' His eyes twinkled as if he understood how fine the line can be between showing confidence and faking it, without being scared out of your wits yourself. There were boundaries, which should not be crossed. One of them was not swearing in front of the crew. He was right, of course. The sailors expected better from future officers. It was a sensible bit of mentoring advice.

I left for my break, hearing George singing a rendition of South Pacific—

'Some enchanted evening,
Someone maybe laughing.
You may hear her laughing
—across a crowded room.'

Where Mr Thompson failed in his ironmonger's shop ashore I felt George might pursue a singing career.

I took a mug of coffee on to the deck outside my cabin, and watched the wooden slatted pilot ladder jumping, twisting, like a white snake uncoiling from a tree, before settling snugly against the ship's side. Minutes later the pilot cutter, bow slicing out a white plume came into view. Not waiting to see the pilot board, I returned my mug to the mess room and made for the wheelhouse, slipping in moments before the pilot. He confidently strode across to greet Captain Smith who was standing with both hands on the ledge of the wheelhouse window. 'How are you Captain—good trip?' asked the pilot, reaching across to shake hands. He was six foot tall, with windswept blond hair, red cheeked, wearing a blue windcheater and yellow scarf. Captain Smith removed his right hand from the ledge to clasp the pilot's outstretched palm, a relieved smile on his face. 'Good to be back in "home" piloted waters, though Paul,' he said.

The home piloted waters identifying memories of the ship in the river Parana. A buoy was out of position, although the Argentinean river pilot insisted it wasn't. We then ploughed into mud. Captain Smith raced across and swung the telegraph to stop. Then got on the phone to the engine room. 'Second Engineer I need full astern to get clear of a mud bank, but shut down as soon as possible, when the telegraph moves to stop.' He then rang full astern. The torque of the propeller made the ship shudder as if being shaken by a giant. The stern mast's top flipped back and forth shaking like a baby's rattle. The engine's energy vibrated through the floor of the wheelhouse. Bridge doors jumped in their mountings. The power thrust arcing the length of the ship. In the quiet of the river, the engine noise, like the roar of an enraged animal. As the propeller battled to pull the bow away the Mate made for the foredeck, waving his arms, to signal release from the mud. Captain Smith standing by the telegraph rang for stop engines. Immediately he rang for slow then half speed ahead, worried that Albany Princess half full of grain would plough into the opposite bank. While this was going on the Argentine pilot lit a cigarette and retired to the far corner of the bridge. Had this release not been achieved by the Captain tugs would have been called out from Buenos Aires. The company would not have been pleased with the delay and extra cost. The Buenos Aires Lloyds surveyor, passed the ship as seaworthy, but nevertheless a dry dock inspection in Tilbury was decided upon.

# Captain Smith Asks Paul Anderson About His Wife and Daughter

It was apparent that they knew each other, that is Captain Smith and the Pilot, because he addressed the Pilot as Paul. While waiting for the windlass to lift the anchor, they stood just in front of the wheel. I couldn't help but overhear the conversation. 'Is she really twenty two now? It doesn't seem possible that you and Natalia have been married that long. Are they alike? That dark Spanish hair, bright blue eyes. Remember the look in your eyes when Natalia teased you. Saying, that she inherited the blue eyes from a Scottish grandfather working on the railways in Buenos Aires. Didn't expect that, did you Paul?' The Pilot raised a pair of binoculars to his eyes before calmly saying, 'No, Jane has blue green eyes and blond hair. She takes after my side of the family.'

That was the only part of the conversation I heard, because the f 'o'c'sl'e bell rang rapidly signalling that the anchor was aweigh from the sea bed. The Pilot was under orders now and his main focus on safely navigating the ship into port. A ship's Captain having ultimate responsibility for the ship, save in the Panama Canal, where canal operators take full control. In this situation Captain Smith was relaxed. Only lighting the occasional cigarette. The Pilot paced the length of the wheelhouse and out on the bridge, noting the Giro Compass reading before calling for '—Slow Ahead,' followed some seconds later by '—Half speed, ten degrees port helm.' The ship was pointed seawards and the bow needed swinging around toward shore and the buoyed channel.

As the bow swept round, engine noise from the funnel, would one moment increase, then get left behind. A rise and fall of sound. The determined click of the giro compass, registered rapid course alteration. 'Mid-ships, Mid-ships, now Quartermaster, if you please,' the Pilot called out returning from inspecting the ship's circling progression from the far side of the bridge. 'Mid-ships, Pilot,' I said, allowing the spoke handles on the wheel to feed through my hands until the dial was at zero, and the brass capped handle of the wheel uppermost. I appreciated the blast of warm air from the air conditioning blower, now both bridge doors were open. The Giro compass clicked like a metronome through a hundred degrees. The Pilot decreased speed to slow ahead and ordered ten degrees starboard helm, stalling the rapid bow swing to port. He stood by the Giro compass, which was slowly coming down from a course of 110 degrees.

'—Steady on 096 degrees Quartermaster, as she settles,' he said. '—Steadying on 096 degrees, pilot,' I replied, and not long after I followed with '—steady on 096 degrees now, pilot.' He acknowledged by raising his left hand after adjusting engine speed from half to full ahead. Almost immediately following with '—Stop Engines. The Third Mate, on the bridge, was not anticipating this, he slipped on the deck before grabbing the outer telegraph handle on the bridge. 'Engine's stopped,' he spluttered, swinging the lever back to stop. The pilot looked through the open door, turned and said, quietly, 'Thank you, Mr Mate,' the Third not realizing how close the pilot was. Captain Smith entered the wheelhouse from the chart room. The sudden stopping of the main engine, no doubt alerting him to changed circumstances.

# Chapter 6

# Dockside — an Ambulance Arrives

'The ferry's decided to take a short cut across the entrance channel. I've stopped engines to allow it across, Captain,' said the pilot walking out on to the bridge. Captain Smith picked up a pair of binoculars and trained them on a small funnelled vessel ahead out to starboard. 'No problem Paul, I've just heard the company's not paying off until tomorrow morning. There's an office party apparently. Never mind the ship's been at sea for three weeks. Look at that, the passengers are all along the port side. They must think we've stopped, just so they can get a better look.' 'That's quite possible,' said the pilot.

The ferry scuttled across in front of us, passengers waving. It crossed my mind that George might be waving back on the Monkey Island. Even acting out singing a song. 'Not able to maintain course easily, now pilot,' I said. We must have been almost stopped in the water. 'Okay, thank you Quartermaster.—Slow Ahead Mr Mate, now.' The Third already by the telegraph, called back—'Slow Ahead, pilot.' We moved to half speed.

Shortly afterwards the pilot said, 'They're waiting for us,' and 'Stop Engines.' Identical looking tugs. One with Mersey Lady painted in white on the bow, the other with just the name Mary, were waiting either side of the channel. Black and white smoke poured out of tall, wire stayed, black and red funnels. They steamed towards us. Mersey Lady, threw a weighted line on to the foredeck to take a wire towing spring. Tug boat Mary would steam to the stern and take aboard a large sisal rope. Soon we were passing cranes and ships alongside warehouses. The fresh sea air taken out by the oil, smoke, smell of Liverpool dockland. The Pilot turned the ship in the basin.

The tugs, pressed their coir fender bows against the ship's side, and with engines racing pushed to assist us alongside.

Customs Officers were crawling over the ship when I met up with Tom in the dining saloon for lunch. The saloon consisted of a long table opposite three smaller ones. The more junior ranks sat at a long table. The bulkheads (walls) polished pine and mahogany. The senior officers tables allowed a panoramic view of the after deck. Tom and myself sat opposite each other by the door. Wann the Hong Kong Chinese steward came across with the menu. 'It is good to be on dry land Mr Tom, Mr Mike. My job much better.' 'We're not on dry land Wann,' said Tom. 'You know what Wann means. He's saying the ship's no longer affected by the sea. I think that's a good way of putting it.' Wann gave me a smile, unseen by Tom as he held the menu in front of his eyes, before ordering vegetable soup. 'Any chance of some more bread rolls?' 'Maybe, in a few minutes Mr Tom. Chief Steward still in galley. When he leave okay-ee.' 'You're a pal Wann.'

Both Wann and Tom were contracted to stay on board in the UK. Tom was helping him learn Spanish, which contributed to our getting well looked after in the dining saloon. Born in Rosario, Argentina. Father British, mother Argentinean, Tom was sent to school in England. He spoke fluent Castilian Spanish, but with his background understood Castilgano, which was the Argentinean dialect. The First Mate valued this ability, when the ship was in Argentina. Tom would say, 'Only speak English, no comprende senor,' to the stevedores.

I was always saying that. This encouraged them to babble away not realizing Tom understood every word. He then informed the Mate of a potential fight or when overhearing a scheme to thieve cargo.

'Mike you're back home—look happy,' Tom said. 'I bet the first words I hear will be when are you going back,' I replied. Although not long a seaman I understood how your life was seen as exotic by those with office jobs, which it was in terms of the countries visited. While they stopped work on Friday you continued round the clock, but this was not considered. Unintentionally perhaps implying your leave was too long. Far longer sometimes than their annual fortnight holiday. Your working life considered more holiday than work.

You might take a girl out, but it could be deflating when told, 'Of course I'd never marry a sailor, who was away for months or years'. 'Feel sorry for me' continued Tom, 'I'm in this strange land, where there's no immediate threat of arrest by the Argentinean military. People are not disappearing from the streets. It rains almost constantly and depressingly I have to stay on board, while everyone else goes on leave.'

The cosmopolitan modern European city appearance of Buenos Aires disguised the brutal regime which plucked hundreds off the streets. It was years later that the outside world learned how these people were flung alive from cargo planes into the sea. There was an arrangement. The Mate allowed Tom to stay with his parents in Rosario and take leave owing, in Argentina, provided the time was made up in the UK. We were the last two in the dining saloon, that is except for Wann.

'When's signing off likely to be?' I asked. 'Not of great interest to me', said Tom. 'Or me,' said Wann as he cleared the adjoining table. 'My home Hong Kong. I am foreigner, like Mr Tom.' Wann saved up his leave by remaining on board and then worked as a laundryman aboard a tanker going to Hong Kong. Another Chinese steward, finishing his leave would take over Wann's job on the tanker, while he visited his family. Tom told me about this arrangement. 'I'm not a foreigner, Wann and I'm not sure you are either.......Oh, never mind,' said Tom, turning back to answer my question. 'I heard the Chief Steward ordering his taxi for three tomorrow afternoon when I went past his cabin, which suggests the signing off will be tomorrow morning. You're staying over 'til Sunday, aren't you, Mike?' 'It's been cleared with the Mate?' 'He never said no, when I asked. You, were—there,' said Tom. Signing off was due it seemed Saturday morning.

'You're all right for a visit to aunt and uncle, like when we last hit Liverpool?'—'If the Mate let's me off early Saturday.' Tom was still working, but I got the impression the relief Mate, around the coast took pity on him. All the regular crew save for Tom and Wann went on leave. Not a great deal of work was demanded of Tom, although he wouldn't admit it. 'Yes, you promised your father you'd visit, and they're your only relatives in the UK,' I said. Aunt Hilda and Uncle Fred were into religion, which Tom found challenging to say the least.

Breaking into the quiet of the saloon came the wail of a siren. We both got up and looked out of a window overlooking the dock. It was an ambulance, now stopped some feet from the gangway. The siren died. The ambulance crew tumbled out, then flung open the back doors to get out a stretcher. They ran across to the gangway with the stretcher still folded. Wann came out of the galley. 'What is now happening, is there a fire, what is happening?' asked Wann. 'Don't know Wann,' I said. 'No alarms are sounding on board. Perhaps a stevedores been badly injured.' We returned to our chairs, Wann served us with a sweet and then went to look out of the window. Soon he was waving his serving cloth up and down, excitedly. 'It is the Captain he strapped on stretcher thing. The Second, he help.' We pushed back our chairs and rushed to the window, not seeing the stretcher until the Second Steward stepped on to the gangway, assisting the first stretcher bearer to change to a forward facing position. It was only when they reached the quay and the stretcher levelled out, that we could see it was definitely Smithy.

# Chapter 7

# Mr Thompson Takes Command

We knew it must be serious, but there were tasks to complete after the midday meal. The first that of checking that all lines running ashore were rat guarded—half circles of aluminium drawn together around the warp tied on with cord. Rats attempting high wire act descents to the quay, foiled when faced by a circle of metal. These guards were lashed around all ropes and wires. I inclined to thinking that it could equally protect the ship from rats scurrying up the ropes, as much as protecting the dock area. Tom and I did catch rats at sea by placing cage traps in mast hold locker spaces. Inevitably we met with success with the amount of grain and cattle feed on board. Ship's rats are smaller than land rats, but fierce critters all the same.

Heavy green plastic covers needed hauling over lifeboats and tying down to protect the boats from airborne dirt and dock fumes. Compass binnacles covered and equipment locked away. Tom reported back to the First Mate on the main deck, who was with the stevedore manager. We waited while he talked to the Stevedore Manager at Number One and Two Holds. Tarpaulins were stripped back with the middle sections of the wooden hatches removed. Each opening had a large tube plunged in the grain, sucking it to the silo above. Wire stays held the tubes in position. The Mate turned to Tom. 'Are the covers on the lifeboats?' 'Yes, sir and the rat guards are in place, bridge equipment locked away. 'In that case, you can keep an eye on proceedings on deck, but be available if I need you.'

'How is the Captain, sir?' asked Tom. 'It sounds like a heart attack. The Second Steward found him lay on the carpet in his cabin, breathing, but unconscious. He placed the Captain in the recovery position and stayed with him, shouting for the Chief Steward to call an ambulance.' 'I'm sorry to hear that Mr Mate. It's not sounding good for Captain Smith,' said the stevedore manager, removing his black trilby. 'We saw the stretcher going down the gangway, sir, I hope it's not serious.' 'We can only hope for the best—The ship being in port, rather than at sea, means he'll be getting expert medical attention at the hospital. Should anyone come aboard asking to see Captain Smith direct them to me. We're expecting the company superintendent. Everything is to proceed as normal.' 'Right sir,' said Tom.

Mr Thomson would have taken over, if the Captain became ill or died at sea. He held a Master's Certificate. This ensured the chain of command could immediately pass to a qualified deck officer. Deck officers on British ships then mainly held a certificate one above their actual rank. Second Mates obtained a Master's Certificate, on occasion, before promotion to First Mate.

The tarpaulin was still on Number Three hatch. We went to the accommodation deck to get a better view of the grain extraction operation.

'On my first return to Liverpool I was standing like you Mike, looking down at grain being extracted from Number Three Hold. The grain shifted and the handle of a knife appeared stuck in the back of a body. More of the body appeared as the grain fell away. The part of the blade not in his back glinted in the sunlight. The hunched body fell forward, knocking the handle of the shovel downwards, The silver blade jumped upwards, as if he was making a final push into the grain,' said Tom. 'Gruesome.' 'It was I suppose. There he was stabbed and left in the cascading grain, probably suffocating before dying, I just thought it could be a near perfect crime. The crime scene now thousands of miles away'.

'What happened?' I asked. 'That was sort of hilarious, because there were shouts of "call an ambulance," but then there was an argument about calling the police first. Both came, but it became a scene of crime incident, with the stevedores threatening not to work on the ship. It was one of their own—even though Argentinean. "How many bodies are there?" they were asking. There was only the one, but they quickly returned when offered double money for the remainder of the week.' 'Thanks Tom, for that,' I said. 'I'll think about that stabbing the next time there's a flare up—when I'm down a hold with a gang of stevedores.'

# Chapter 8

# Fall Out with Aunt Hilda

Signing off was on Saturday as Tom deduced from listening to the Chief Steward's ordering of a taxi. I queued in the seaman's mess signing for money owing after deductions, which was a sobering experience. I determined there and then to lock the notes in my desk draw, all bar three pound notes. Climbing up the inner accommodation stairs to the mid deck, I met the Mate, with an A4 size envelope in his hand. 'I've been informed by your mate that you've asked to stay over another day, is that right?' It wasn't how I would have put it, but answered, 'Yes, sir,' to his question. 'It's lonely for him with all of us departing to go to our homes. I expect you were thinking that?' The Mate described concern for Tom's well-being to me, at a higher level than I would have put it. 'Tom took me to see friends and relatives in Argentina, and I agreed as sort of a payback, that I would stay to go ashore, if we were here for Saturday,' which was untrue, but I wasn't going to say it was the result of a bet. 'That's good, I expect he's in need of some relaxation, after completing these—that's all right by me.' The Mate held up the package and I realized that it must be Tom's completed correspondence course work. 'If I don't see you again, have a good leave.' 'And you sir,' I replied, continuing along the corridor to my cabin—not realizing, at that time, how lucky, we were as apprentices having Mr Thomson, as First Mate.

Partly, Tom wanted me to stay, because his father insisted he visit his aunt and uncle, and didn't want to go alone. 'You know how scary they are Mike, you wouldn't leave me to visit on my own,' was how Tom put it, looking at me as if in need of protection from monsters. I visited aunt and uncle with

Tom, when I first joined the ship. They were a trifle eccentric, perhaps. Tom harboured a pathological fear of them, like another might of spiders. It was because they were highly religious.

That Saturday afternoon we stepped off the bus stop, three doors down from their semi. I remembered on the previous visit they were denouncing large material possessions.

When we walked up to the house, this time, their A35 car was abandoned in the driveway, visibly rusting. The end of the world stipulated on the previous visit for 10th December, 1965—an impetus perhaps to give up on material possessions. Tom stepped inside the porch and tapped the door knocker. 'Come in you two out of the wet,' said Aunt Hilda, after opening the door. We did get to sit in the front room, after removing coats and shoes. 'You have been reading those scripture tracts and praying, regularly Thomas?' Asked his aunt, who looked severe, with her greying hair tied back in a bob. Tom was given these on the first visit, but they ended up in a bin. 'I've been busy catching up on course work coming back aunt, but I started praying again when we hit a storm going out. I was nearly thrown from my bunk.' 'That's only praying for yourself,' 'I prayed for the ship, actually aunt.' 'That's better then.'

After aunt went to prepare tea the conversation developed, away from religion with uncle Fred asking about his elder brother, Tom's dad. The subject of religion and morality returned with a vengeance after the tea trolley was wheeled in. 'You'll not be going to the pubs around here, will you?' asked Aunt Hilda, as she placed cake, sandwiches, paper napkins and plates on to the card table, looking back and forth as she spoke to include me in the question. They lived adjacent to the docks—the proximity of pubs conflicting with their religious view. A bit like a couple knowingly buying a house next to a school playground and then complaining about the noise during break time. 'Dens of iniquity,' she continued. 'Magnets for the immoral and degenerate.' They purportedly did not drink.

Tea was being handed around in cups and saucers. Apart from spam and cheese sandwiches, the main feature was a chocolate cake. Aunt made a class cake and we might have been offered a second slice, but Tom upset the tea party at this point. 'Probably a better state of affairs than Narvik. One Norwegian lass serviced twenty sailors from the ore carrier I was on at the time. They could have done with a few more pubs. The Liverpool pub scene probably meets the needs of the area better,' Tom said in a casual sort of way. I spluttered on my remaining bit of cake. What was Tom doing? 'I'd rather you didn't talk of such matters Thomas,' said aunt.

We did not get offered a second cup. Shortly afterwards she started clearing the cups, saucers and plates, back on to the trolley, placing the cake on the lower deck. I later blamed Tom for causing an upset, leading to the cake being taken away. 'They got my goat,' he said. 'I just couldn't take any more of the sermonising.' Tom gave aunt and uncle a half carton of cigarettes (100) on leaving, which appeared to finally cool the situation. Aunt said she would offer up prayers for us, Tom having reaffirmed aunt's opinion that we were in desperate need of saving—yet again.

# Chapter 9

# Back On Board to Get Ready for the Electric Hall

'You knew how your aunt would react, mentioning the bar girl in Narvik. Now we've missed the meal on board,' I said to Tom as we neared the gangway. A tidy quantity of grain would have been discharged, it was now at a steeper angle. The banging of wooden hatches could be heard as we climbed the aluminium steps. 'I can only take so much. I just wanted to get away,' said Tom. Forward from mid-deck four stevedores were standing on top of Number One Hold, dragging the tarpaulin across. At Number Three, a pair of stevedores, were lifting hatches on to the metal support beams to cover the hold. The outer ones in place they needed to stack others on top to fill across the open space to the middle. This led to a continual rat a tat of wood on wood. The main deck was a mess.

The engine room door held ajar made the generator sound loud. Our cabins were opposite. Plus there was a banging from and fitters at work in the engine room. 'Quick, quick, very quick now,' Wann called down the corridor. 'Dinner over in saloon, but have kept for you, salad, and sweet. Peaches okay, ice cream—no okay.' He raised his hand to beckon. 'Come very quick. Chief Steward see, he not like me—again.' 'You're a pal Wann, you're definitely on my Christmas card list' called out Tom 'Wann no have Christmas card celebration,' he said, quizzically. 'Never mind, Wann, never mind, anyway, thanks, we'll be straight in,' said Tom. I was happy about this. I didn't fancy going ashore next time on a near empty stomach—Not then a convert to the glass of milk putting a lining on your stomach.

'Mike you'll have to lend me a tie,' said Tom, after the meal. A knock back pong of Old Spice hit my cabin space as he entered 'Yep, okay, but I want it back,' I said, breaking off from shaving by the washstand. Tom was already into the wardrobe. The tie request could be seen as a compliment for having accompanied him to see aunt and uncle. It was like belated applause that Tom requested to borrow a tie. Affirmation of gratitude displayed in borrowing something, from me, then to be included in the world of Tom. Bathing in the glow of his possible approval was short lived, however. 'God, Mike your ties are dull as ditch water. Here's a yacht club tie. I didn't know you were a yachtie Mike?' 'Leave off, Tom. I can imagine you belonging to a club.' 'A night club, perhaps. Are you part of the County Set then?' 'No, don't be daft, I was born in a seaside town, belonging to a yacht club is no big deal.' It went quiet for a while.

'At last, a tie that looks passable and doesn't look like I'm going to a church funeral. I'll take it off inside anyway.' 'What's the fuss,' then, I said. 'You could stand outside a dance hall stark naked, but so long as you're wearing a tie they'd let you in,' said Tom. 'I don't believe that, they'd call the cops before that happened—by the way,' I continued, 'minutes ago the Third Mate asked if we're going ashore?' Tom's face appeared to lose animation as he interpreted this information. 'What did you say to him?' he asked, letting go the tie as he wound the knot. 'No worry, I told him your aunt and uncle were taking us to see "The Great Escape" at the flicks.' 'He swallowed that?'

'Yes,' I said buttoning up my shirt, as if it was an everyday occurrence, managing to put the Third Mate off from joining us ashore. 'I don't often say this about a junior apprentice, but you're a genius, Mike. At least tonight anyway.' This good news speeded up Tom's getting ready and within fifteen minutes we were locking our cabin doors. The Third Mate was no fun to be ashore with. It started out friendly enough, but he drank beer with chasers and then talked about his marriage, and what was wrong with it. This escalated as the drink took hold. He usually advertised the fact that we were deck apprentices and he was an officer. Tom's guiding principle was to keep quiet about advertising our connection with ships.

Basically the Third messed up our bird pulling chances, as Tom succinctly put it. My view was that we might as well have gone ashore with the word "Merchant Seaman" stamped on our heads. A deep black tan in October, was a giveaway for starters. A breeze from the dock blew across the embarkation deck as we stepped outside. I felt the fibrous tautness of the rope rail, against my hands, as we scuttled down the gangway, shoes clipping the aluminium steps.

# Chapter 10

# Meeting Jane and Christina

I looked back at Albany Princess as we walked toward the dock gates. After the bright lights of the ship we were plunged into the dark and quiet of the docks. The police were employed specifically for guarding the dock area. Dressed in dark blue with helmets like conventional civilian police.

'What ship are you lads from?' The call came across as we neared the gates. 'Albany Princess,' replied Tom. 'These gates close at midnight. You'll need identity to get back in again. Thought about that have you?' Asked the uniformed policeman. 'Not exactly, but we intend getting back before then,' said Tom. 'Make it for eleven thirty—half an hour earlier than Cinderella and I'll let you through. I finish at eleven forty five. 'Thanks for that,' said Tom. 'Reasonably sober. I'm not fishing you out of the dock mind,' he continued. 'We'll manage that,' 'Thanks sergeant,' I said, noting the three silver stripes on his arm.

It was a ten minute walk to the bus stop, around the perimeter of the high wired fence surrounding that part of the dock. Tom knew Liverpool well from his previous stays on ships. I saw the dance hall from the top of the double decker as we approached. The red "Electric Hall" sign written out in tubular neon strips, surrounded by a circular white outer strip. After stepping down from the bus it was a short walk to the Hall. Two bouncers stood outside, incongruous in dinner jackets and bow ties. Their bulk and misshapen noses testimony to a boxing career or punch ups. I did not ask which. They looked us up and down, checking for the wearing of ties as Tom mentioned earlier. 'Evening gentlemen, entrance price is five shillings. Tickets available inside, no smoking in the dance hall and you may be asked to leave the premises at management's discretion,' the nearest one said. The other followed up with, 'Have a good evening, gentlemen,' in a more welcoming tone.

We individually paid the entrance fee at the ticket office. Tom said, 'The no smoking request is a code for no fighting or disruption. I've seen them in action when there's unwanted behaviour. They're quick to break it up.' 'Don't think I'll bother starting a fight then,' I said, handing my the ticket to the green coated usherette at the bar door. The clinking of glasses and chatter swept towards us on entering. No one noticed , save a white aproned barman. He looked across while waiting for a glass to fill from a tap. Tom ahead of me called back 'Look, look Mike, there's Christina, the Third's daughter sat over there. The one with black hair opposite the blond. I'm sure it's her. The hair's shorter, but it's the Third's daughter. You remember the photo you asked about on his desk?' I was unconvinced. 'I'm sure it is. There's one way to find out. Here Mike get two halves.' Tom removed a pound note from his wallet. A roll on the drums came from the stage, which stopped talk momentarily from customers, waiting to be served two deep, around the bar.

I left Tom, introducing himself to the two girls. The dark haired girl smiled and the blond didn't seem to mind the intrusion. Tom was a social animal. I used to believe it was the age difference of nearly two years between us. I have to admit he could easily strike up a conversation. Good at working a room of total strangers, if need be. A useful attribute for, not least, a Captain entertaining aboard ship. Tobacco smoke, made visible by spotlights in the bar canopy, swirled about in a drift.

The disc jockey's microphone boosted voice, followed another roll on the drums, 'There here folks, the best band playing L'pool tonight. They're here to make you twist the night away. Liverpool's answer to Chubby Checker.' The disembodied voice flowed into the bar as the doors leading into the dance floor opened.

# Chapter 11

# Missed Opportunity

I looked across while attempting to carry the mugs of beer without spilling the contents to where Tom was now sat next to the dark haired girl. The blond beckoned for me to sit next to her, an amused look on her face. Tom oblivious to my return carried on talking.

'Aren't you going to introduce us Tom?' the blond raised her voice above the babble from the bar area. This refined English type of voice made Tom break away from his chat, trying to catch what she was saying—above the music from the dance hall. 'Well done sport,' he said, as I reached across with the glass of beer. A term of address adopted by Tom when we were ashore. 'Jane, Christina meet Mike,' Tom waved his hand first to Jane, Christina and finally me. Christina gave me one of those just above the table waves with her right hand. Jane said, 'Hi Mike,' as I sat next to her. 'Mike's not from Liverpool.' 'There's a surprise I'd never have guessed that, would you Jane?' I wondered if Christina was as Tom imagined from the photograph. I saw the likeness now. 'Didn't expect to see my dad's ship mates here. Are there any others?' she asked looking around. 'Not as far as we know,' said Tom. That may have been a disappointment to Christina, but the last thing we wanted was to meet up with the crew. Jane turned towards me 'Your ship docked on Friday didn't it Mike?' 'How did you know that?' I asked. 'My father was the pilot, that's how I know.'

My call of—'Hey Tom, you know Jane's father piloted the ship in,' was drowned out by the scraping of chairs as Christina and Tom stood up—Tom not exactly in a hurry. 'Come on Tom anyone can do the Twist. It's not ballroom,' said Christina grabbing his arm to encourage more of a response. Neither of them hearing what I said. We did know that Christina was a nurse. Nurses and merchant seaman nearly always seemed to hit it off. Perhaps because of working in a similar hierarchical structure of chiefs and Indians.

A hospital also having complementary occupations working together as on board a ship.

'Did you meet my father then?' Jane said, turning her chair to the side, while uncrossing endless looking tanned legs. 'Yes, I was the wheelman. They were talking about you,' 'Nothing too awful,' she said pulling a face. 'No, the Captain asked how old you were.' 'And my father told him that?' 'Yes, twenty two.' 'I'll have words with him. Giving away my age to all and sundry. Do I look twenty two?' This was getting a bit tricky. I took a sip of my beer before replying. 'I thought you were the same age as Tom, when I first came in. Both you and Christina. That's nineteen.' That met with approval. 'Christina will be pleased she's nearly twenty three. You were on the bridge then all the time going into port. I'm jealous,' she said.

I wasn't sure how to take this remark. Uncertain how my position on board was able to elicit jealousy. 'I'd love to be an apprentice on board a ship,' she exclaimed, making me realize Tom must have put out our roles as apprentices on general release. 'What do you do then? I asked. 'I work at a bank, which is boring and repetitive and Christina has just qualified as an SRN. 'What's that?' I asked. 'A State Registered Nurse. Don't you know that? Father talks about his time at sea. He used to work for Blue Circle Line, the same company as you work for—before becoming a pilot. He mentioned about bringing Smithy in on Albany Princess yesterday. 'You call him Smithy? like we do on board.' 'He was First Mate and father Second when my mother came back as a passenger from Rosario, where she was born. She talks about her childhood living on an estancia all those years ago. Granny Sofia came to visit recently. My mother's dream is to go back to Argentina to visit her sister Rayen and her two brothers. Tom comes from Rosario.' 'Does he really,' said Jane, 'I don't actually know Captain Smith, but father will say to mother, Smithy's back. 'I've got some bad news.' 'What's that?' 'Captain Smith was taken ashore on a stretcher. Taken to hospital in an ambulance.'

'They'll be upset. When did this happen Mike?' 'Yesterday afternoon. We were in the dining saloon, when the ambulance arrived. The First Mate told us he thought it was a heart attack.'

Jane, for me was definitely the most attractive girl at the Electric Hall that Saturday evening. At my age then and the fact that she was the pilot's daughter and more sophisticated than your average girl meant I was more than a bit in awe. 'I hope he's all right,' she said. 'Yes, he was talking about retiring to a cottage in Devon, during the trip.' She picked up her wine glass by the stem to take a sip. There was a pause in the conversation. I noticed men at the bar behind looking across.

There was a noisy office type party in progress on the far side, but it was Jane who was getting their attention, although she made out not to notice. 'You'll be going on leave then Mike?' 'Tomorrow yes,' I replied. She moved her chair backwards, revealing again legs well equipped for wearing a short skirt. She was both attractive and friendly. 'Tom takes his leave in Rosario,' I continued. 'Is that to be with his family?' 'Yes, we signed off yesterday but I said I'd stay a day longer. He visits an aunt and uncle and doesn't like going on his own. I lost a bet on the day we docked. I said I'd stay to go to the dance, instead of going home. Tom said there's more chance to...' 'Pick up birds?' she said. Her face crinkled into a smile. I'd walked into that one 'My mother talks about wanting to revisit Rosario,' she continued, not phased by my gaucheness 'They might know each other's families, then,' I said. 'Does Tom have other relatives here?' 'I don't know,' which was true. You can get all sorts of questions from a girl, not necessarily a good sign when they're asking more about your mate than they are about you. 'It's not that exactly, but they get him rattled, being very religious. Heck I sound like a parent or guardian.' 'You're mates aren't you. Father talks about his life as an apprentice. There's just the two of you. You work together. Look after each other, buddies. At first, I wasn't sure whether Tom was an apprentice. I though perhaps he was Third Mate.' 'He'd like that,' I said. 'Tom thinks it's best not to say that we're apprentices or even from a ship.' 'The first thing he said to us was that he was from the Albany Princess, which docked on Friday.'

This was getting tricky, but I decided to explain. 'The Third Engineer has a photo of Christina on his desk. Tom recognized Christina when we first came in. I'm not sure I should be telling you this. She's younger in the photo. I didn't believe him when he said Christina was the girl in the photo.' 'And my father was the pilot on your ship, yesterday. It seems more than a coincidence for the four of us to meet.' I didn't mention that Tom came hoping to find Christina at the Electric Hall.

A couple walked by heading for the dance floor followed by a man chatting to the pair. He broke away and came across to where we were sitting. 'Would you like to dance? 'He smiled knelt down toward Jane holding out his hand. 'My friend's with his girlfriend. I saw you arrive earlier with your friend and I'm on my own.' A little dog lost appeal transmitting from his eyes. Sick making, but not it appeared to Jane. 'Can you watch the coats and handbags Mike?' She said, standing up and smiling at him before leaving for the dance floor. I just nodded and said, 'Okay.' Why wouldn't she dance when asked by this man? I was younger than her and already flattered by the attention. That did not prevent me feeling a sense of loss. Certainly lost opportunity. Why hadn't I asked Jane to dance! There was no language barrier. Tom might say that there was a cultural one. That Jane was in effect out of my league.

# Chapter 12

# Tom Arranges to Meet Christina

Apart from a few couples arriving, the bar area was all but clear. It was as if a flight departure from an airport lounge had been called. The foyer bar was similarly vacated. The first time that, Courage, Watney's Red Barrel, Whitbread and the two taps for draught Guinness were visible at the bar. One covered with a bar towel to denote that the barrel was empty.

The music stopped, but the loud voices and laughter magnified as the door opened from the dance floor opposite to where I was sitting. In the crowd I recognized Tom's voice and heard him say to Christina. 'Look Mike's all on his own.' 'Jane's dancing, I'm looking after the coats.' I said hastily as they arrived at the table, before Tom was able to make some remark about me being slow off the mark. 'Tom can do that now. I want to dance,' Christina said evidently enjoying herself.

I was loving it someone ordering Tom about. I took the hint getting to my feet. 'Christina will you, I mean can I have the next dance?' 'Mike I really wanted to dance with you, but couldn't get you away from Jane.' Her eyes flashed at Tom but got no response. It was in all possibility a lie, but I didn't mind. 'Change, sport,' said Tom, holding out his hand. I'd not forgotten. Christina dragged Tom away before there was a chance to hand it over. I handed back a ten shilling note two half crowns and some small change. Tom made a bee line for the now vacant bar. 'He wants a drink, I want to dance, so come on Mike.'

Christina led the way across the bar to the dance floor through the double doors and into the more subdued lighting of the dance floor—spotlights directed on to the stage area.

'They're back, fully lubricated and ready to get you twisting, The Mersey Shakers, Ladies and Gentlemen,' the disc jockey announced—prominent in a bright yellow and pink shirt. A spotlight picked out an enlarged photo of a beach, sea and sky on the wall behind. Artificial tropical palms doted around the perimeter of the podium, attempted to create a Hawaiian holiday effect. Several pairs of girls were picking up their handbags and leaving, when the lights went out around the turntables, and the disc jockey took a break. Christina led the way over to that area of the dance floor.

'Do you have a girlfriend then Mike?' She lent towards me as we twisted our feet and legs to the groups demands of "Twist Again Like We Did Last Summer." 'Sort of,' I said, 'but it's not easy to keep a relationship going when you're away for three months at a time.' The record ended and the next one was a slow waltz, which brought us close. I could see Jane leaving the floor, but not with her dance partner. It looked as though she decided on the one dance. I was fast realizing, I cared about Jane. Christina noticed me looking across. 'Hey you're dancing with me Mike, not my flat mate.' I felt the heat in my face. I'm glad my sun tanned face covered what would have been blushing embarrassment. 'I'm going on leave tomorrow,' I said as if that had any relevance.

After the dance we returned to where Jane and Tom were sitting in the bar area. 'You haven't fallen out with Christine have you,' said Tom. 'Jane says she's just turned down an offer of marriage on the dance floor.' 'No, I didn't,' said Jane.' 'Are you both married then?' he asked. The Electric Hall was that kind of place, where marrieds might pretend they were still foot loose and fancy free, although this did not cross my mind with Jane and Christina. 'Well are you?' persisted Tom, which came across as rude. 'Does it matter?' Asked Christina. She placed her left hand on the table. There was a green stoned ring on the third finger. 'You're not wearing a wedding ring.'

'We find it a bit restrictive when we're out on the town, don't we Chris?' said Jane. Christina pursed her lips, and nodded her head in agreement. 'We look like married women to you then?' said Christina turning to look directly at Tom. 'That's not very flattering is it Jane?' she said pulling a face. Both laughed. 'You told me you're being picked up later and not staying late.' said Tom. 'We're being picked up by Jane's dad in twenty minutes, not our husbands or boyfriends. Fooled you though,' said Christina.

I wasn't sure how Tom was going to take this, but selected the moment to ask Jane, if she wanted to dance. 'They're like an old married couple already Mike. Perhaps we'd better leave them to it,' she said, getting up to leave for the dance floor. The misgivings of staying back an extra day now vanished having met Jane and now with an opportunity of being alone with her on the dance floor. We went through the double doors leading to the dance area. Brenda Lee and "Sweet Nuthin" just ended as we reached the floor. Above the noisy chatter came the disc jockey's loud voice. 'Here's Andy, with "Moon River" for all you romantic dreamers and lovers out there. A chance to get up close, folks.' The group were sitting to one side of the stage with pints of beer. The lights dimmed further as the record started. We held hands, before moving close.

I knew I would remember that perfume and forever identify it with Jane, even if we never met again. This was a waltz and I could cope with it. I remember a mischievous look in her eyes as I placed my arm around her waist. She let go of my right hand moving in close. 'Will you be back in Liverpool after your leave?' she asked drawing away. Then getting close again. 'I don't know,' I said, but was already hoping we would be. 'Let me guess where you're from. Somewhere south of here—London?' 'I sound like a Londoner then?' 'You're not from Liverpool'. 'That's right, but further to the South and West. Bridport, in Dorset,' I said. 'That's a very nice county.'

'It's just a town by the sea to me,' I replied, not wanting to talk particularly about my home town, while holding Jane close.

The song ended all too soon. The group were back with a live Twisting number. We parted to do the Twist. Jane skilled with the more advanced leg movements, kicking off her shoes, to achieve this. 'We'll have to get back to the bar, Mike,' she said looking at her watch luminescent in the dark. The lights came up. She picked up her shoes. Nimbly bending each knee to replace them, without losing balance. A skill I knew beyond my capability.

'Hey, you haven't fallen out,' said Tom as we returned to the table. This was appearing to be his stock phrase for the evening. 'Anyway Jane, we thought you'd left us. I was telling Christina, how your dance partner leaves me once he's got a girl of his own.' 'We don't do that do we Jane?' 'Neither do I,' I hastened to add. 'Tom's making that up.' Tom and Christina were on to another round of drinks. Tom's banter suggested he was further ahead in the drink stakes, than the three of us. 'Would you like a drink?' I asked Jane. 'No it's all right Mike. Christina we'd better be going I don't want to have father invading.' They picked up their coats and shoulder bags in preparation to leave.

'It's been nice meeting you two. Might see you next time you're in Liverpool.' said Jane. 'Not sure about that,' said Christina 'I don't see this as long term, spending Saturday evenings here , but hey, you never know.' 'See you soon Tom,' Christina said. She looked at Jane and smiled. They both waved from the door on leaving. 'What does that mean?' 'I asked Christina for a date while you were impressing Jane with your dancing skills,' said Tom, who boasted about having been taught to ballroom dance. 'You're not taking Christina to see aunt and uncle?' 'No, that new film, The Great Escape.

# Chapter 13

# Dry Dock to Cargo Loading

The rail warrant came in the post after a telegram to re-join Albany Princess at Tilbury dry dock.

The ship shored up, deep down in the dry dock. The white superstructure at ground level, gave the impression of some avant-garde hotel, but then interrupted by the large red and black funnel. The ship's whistle appearing larger, than when the ship was afloat. The Klaxon trumpet like a gigantic hunting horn, held out, waiting to rally the hunt with its call. Three brown painted masts stood forlorn, like leafless trees in a strange land. The port lifeboat swung out on the davits to deck level being inspected by two men in white boiler suits. One was writing notes on a clip board, the other pointing to pieces of equipment.

Diesel fumes from a generator, set up alongside the dock , blew across to where I was standing. The pulse of the engine drowning out other sounds. I placed the grip I was holding on the ground to take in the picture. The extraordinary depth of the ship below the waterline was now apparent out of water. There were ladders supporting planks around the ship to work from and wooden props either side of the keel. Men worked below, with Albany Princess, a Gulliver in Lilliput, dwarfing all around.

I spotted Tom mid-ships in a dark blue boiler suit, holding a long bamboo with roller attached. A cigarette nonchalantly dangled from his mouth, indicating that the Mate was probably not yet returned from leave.

'Glad you're back Mike,' Tom said as I approached from the steps leading down into the dry dock. 'It's a new paint we're testing for British Paints. You see the chalk marked plates?

They're the ones that have to be painted with the test paint. It's not got to dry for too long. It's supposed to work better when the salt water gets to it, while damp.'—*No, 'welcome back or how was shore leave?'*—but that was Tom.

'Get your work clothes and we can finish early. Here's my cabin key.' Tom pulled off a glove dripping with red paint, before digging out the key from his pocket and flinging it in my direction. 'There's a Coke for you if you bring me one. They're in a case in the wardrobe.' And finally 'spect you're glad to be back.' 'What makes you think that?' I said. 'I saw you with that girl Jane, your face all lit up. Right little Casanova in the making. We'll probably not see them again, they'll have forgotten us.' 'Thought you were keen on Christina, anyway,' I said. 'Jane's a dream to look at, have to admit. Bit too classy for you Mike.' 'Not for you, then?' 'Does it matter?' I said, 'Our chances of seeing them again are slim'.

Back at the top of the dock the gangway was now a roped walkway, that dipped steeply down to the deck. Saw dust was scattered to soak up pools of spilt oil. flecks of wool and cotton attached to wires and round the mast housings. Tarpaulins roughly thrown on hatches. Metal beams and clumps of timber placed on top to hold them down. The Mate would have fifty fits about the state of the ship when he returned from leave. It was like a pig heap everywhere.

Black flex and light bulbs, with wire guards were strung along the corridor, leading to our cabins. I heard a squeal followed by giggling as I went by the Sixth Engineer's cabin. After changing into work clothes and grabbing two cans of Coke, I returned to the top of the dry dock and made my way back down the tiered steps to where Tom was working. There were unused trays and long rollers nearby. A five gallon drum held the special paint. I unscrewed the cap and struggled to get the right angle for pouring, on to the tray. 'Only half fill that tray,' Tom shouted. 'Okay keep your shirt on,' I called back.

'Hey Scouser where's the Coke then?' For Tom everyone became Scouser once we hit Liverpool, disregarding the fact we were now at Tilbury. Not sure it went down, well being called a Scouser among the engineers , but maybe Tom did it to be provoking. I struggled to get the Coke cans free, from my donkey jacket pockets before handing one to Tom's outstretched, impatient hand. 'The Sixth Engineer's got his girlfriend on board, then,' I said to Tom. 'That's not his girlfriend, she's a tart he picked up at the Kings Arms.' 'How does he get away with that?' I asked. 'He's an engineer Mike, not an apprentice. The Second Engineer turns a blind eye.' The paint roller made a squelching sound as Tom ran it over the ship's plate loaded with the special paint. 'The Second says the Sixth puts in a good day's work, since she's been with him. He's not drinking a case of beer a day. There's just the slanging match next morning over how much he owes for services rendered. She keeps coming back though. Then the ship's on dry land and not going anywhere. Here get that paint roller rolling and let's get finished, Mike.'

Early next day the dry dock was flooded and we were on our way around the coast to the Bristol Channel ports. The cargo there ranged from cases of steel plate, railway lines, crated machinery, cars , tractors, equipment to fit out a hospital, lorry chassis, single decker buses, car body parts for assembly; to smaller items like bags marked with the ICI logo; others filled with China Clay. Barrels of unblended whisky were wedged into place in the four special cargo lockers, together with hundreds of boxes of brandy, whisky, gin and Drambuie. The final voyage around the coast was to Liverpool. The remaining 'tween deck space filled with buses and lorry chassis. Six lorry chassis were securely wired on deck with red drums of ethanol fore and aft the accommodation. The ethanol drums one above another, separated with wooden dunnage, (thin strips of rough timber often with the bark still on the edges) interspersed with vertical planking at the front, and wire strapped. Highly flammable the Ethanol needed to be on deck, but shippers might expect to pay a lower premium for cargo exposed to waves and the elements. On Monday the relief crew left , Mr Thompson, the First Mate returned. Bosun, and deck hands were immediately set to clearing debris. Holds were inspected, before the metal strengthening beams were lowered into position; wooden hatches slotted in and then the three green coverings of tarpaulins hauled across the hatches.

Next day I broke out the Blue Peter flag, furled ready on the Monkey island. It required a sharp tug on the lanyard to release—when unfurled, the fabric made a taut snapping sound in the wind. A dark blue flag with white centre. It was a public signal that the ship was about to sail. Hoisted at sea it meant your lights are out or burning badly. I didn't know how it was seen in the dark though. I fastened the lanyard, while hearing the high revving of a fork lift truck as it came out of a warehouse—unaware that it was preparing to lay a pallet in preparation for passengers luggage. Cargo liners on long haul runs might have up to twelve passenger cabins. The Albany Princess only had six. Two small cabins were set aside for the Stevedore Manager and Tally Clerk. The superstructure was elaborate. It impressed the Argentineans, believing the ship to be more substantial in size when viewed sailing into port or alongside. Dummy windows and portholes were added to suggest the ship was much larger than it really was.

# Chapter 14

# Mr Thomson, the First Mate, Gives a Lecture about Best Practice

I left the Monkey Island after hoisting the Blue Peter, returning to the dining saloon where we were scraping and re-gleeming the floor. In the centre of The floor the tiles were cut to form a star shape. The side nearest the serving hatch was clear of tables and chairs. It meant either being on your hands and knees or kneeling in the process of scraping the frazzled remnants curled up after applying paint stripper.

Tom was brushing the stripper on the tiles well in advance of scraping, otherwise the pungent fumes were likely to make your eyes smart. We were being supervised by Angelo the ship's chippie, who had left us to it. 'This has to be done about every three years,' said Tom. 'Just our bloody luck it's time to do it now,' I replied. 'I don't know, it's better having an indoor job in the UK.' He stood pouring paint stripper on the tiles then rapidly spreading it with a four inch brush, before it congealed and dried. 'It's a darn sight cleaner Mike—warmer than hanging over the side on a painting stage with black paint plastering face and clothes. Tom knelt down and screwed the cap back on the can of paint stripper 'You sound like the Mate,' I said, 'next you'll be calling it a five minute job.' The Mate's five minute job might be painting the funnel, which could take several days.

Tom on his previous ship was the junior of a group of four apprentices. Now the senior apprentice there were occasions when he liked to remind me of his status and experience. This being one of them. The hatch from the Saloon Galley rattled open. A tray with a pot of coffee, milk jug and sugar bowl slid across the pass to the front. 'You lads want a coffee, said the Second Steward peering through the hatch. 'Have you made that for us Sec?' asked Tom. I could see Wann at the sink polishing pots with a yellow duster. His wave and smile, unnoticed by the Second. 'Don't be daft it was the Chief Engineer's, but he was leaving for the engine room You lads might as well have it.' 'Thanks Sec,' said Tom, 'we're about due for a break.' The Second's elbows rested on the hatch, hands supporting his head. No doubt surveying how near we were to completing the Gleeming of the floor. He turned towards where Wann was working, 'Fetch a couple of cups for the apprentices Wann.' 'Yes Mr Second, Wann is now coming with cups,' I heard from the back of the galley. The Second moved away from the hatch as Wann placed two cups on the tray. 'Like very much floor, nearly like new,' said Wann. 'Thanks Wann,' I said as I picked up the tray, glad that someone appreciated our efforts.

Just as we finished the coffee Chippie entered through the saloon door. 'You boys have done well. The Chief wants you to tidy up here. The passengers are due to arrive and he asked for me to release you to help with the baggage. I will complete the rest this afternoon and tomorrow.' We took the scrapers, paint stripper can, and brushes back to the Bosun's locker at the stern of the ship. The smell of the tarred coils of hemp rope, intermingling with the stench of paint and paraffin.

On our way back I saw the Mate standing on number four hatch checking that the metal locking bars were secure. These were like straps you might have around a large suitcase. In this instance they were in place to prevent stormy seas and wind from getting under tarpaulins and ripping them away. Galvanised strips bedded the tarpaulins into metal cleats around the sides and ends of the hatch. Wooden wedges were later hammered in to place, hopefully swelling and gripping even tighter when waves broke across the decks.

As we walked past number five hold the Mate spotted us. He crossed the green tarpaulin atop of Number Four, and jumped cat-like on deck, belying his sixty two years. 'Right, you two. Chips has passed the message on then.' 'Yes sir, we've just been clearing up.' Tom made towards the railings to get rid of his cigarette. 'The Chief Steward has been telephoned by the agent. There are four passengers arriving by taxi plus two crew members. Captain Anderson and his wife will be arriving later. You were on the wheel when we docked lad. You remember the pilot who took us in?'—'Yes sir,' I said. 'Well, he's our new Captain. A former company's man—Paul Anderson won't let much get past him. I agreed with the Chief Steward they'll need to be a general tidying up of language among the crew with women on board this trip. It goes without saying you two will be expected to be on best behaviour. Captain Smith was strict about the wearing of uniform in the dining saloon. Captain Anderson will be wanting a similar standard.'

'When you say women, Chief do you mean women passengers and Mrs Anderson?' 'Yes, Tom Blake, I did mean women passengers—there are two, plus the Captain's wife. Also his daughter and a nurse, who will be working as crew members Captain Anderson's daughter's also working her passage—very brave. I hope she knows what she's letting herself in for. The other's a friend. A nurse, who is to assist a couple related to the owner. Two of the four passengers are folk singers, popular in Buenos Aires, but little known in England.'

Tom looked at me with raised eyebrows. Both of us realizing that the two crew members must be Jane and Christina. 'You'd both better get a shift on. You need to muster in uniform on the gangway in fifteen minutes. The Chief, Second Steward and Wann are assisting the passengers. The two crew members will have the remaining two passenger cabins. You two can assist them. You'd best see the Second

Steward for their keys. Have I made myself clear? Oh yes, They'll be sitting in your group on the main table in the dining saloon. I've got some final adjustments to make on the Rolston. After the evening meal you can bring them to the bridge. Any questions?' 'Will there be much luggage, sir?' asked Tom. Obviously deciding not to let Mr Thomson know that we'd already met Jane and Christina. 'The Bosun's setting up derricks by Number Three. You may be needed to carry luggage to the cabins once the pallet of luggage is on deck. All right you'd better get a move on.'

'Hey Mike,' said Tom, as we walked back along the accommodation deck, '—didn't expect to see Christina and Jane. It's like pre-arranged by the gods. Well for me at any rate. Definitely saw a look of disappointment in her eyes at the cinema after I said we were set to be away for three months. Pity Jane's so attractive, older and out of your league.' Tom knew how to put the boot in. 'Are you saying Christina purposely applied for a job as nurse to be with you?' 'Wait 'til I tell her about Rosa.' A near neighbour in Rosario, who Tom wrote to and I could see him marrying. His mother, said she liked Rosa very much and maybe they'd get engaged. Her father, apparently a manager at the Bank of South America. 'You dare Mike Peters and your life won't be worth living,' he said, taking hold of the elbow sleeve and then the collar of my donkey jacket before making a fist at me in warning. The Rolston Indicator, mentioned by the Mate, was an instrument, modelling the weight distribution of the cargo. With its miniature weights represented the various cargoes loaded. My mind in a diversion escaped into another world of ship's and cargo, momentarily. I then blurted out. 'Hey Tom mate keep your hair on, just joking, that's all.' I said, as he let go of my jacket.

Once it was revealed that Paul Anderson was a former experienced Blue Circle company man I appreciated how the company could see him as a suitable replacement for Captain Smith at short notice. He might have been enticed by the opportunity for his wife Natalia to re-visit Argentina. That Jane was with Christina not that improbable when both had fathers associated with the Blue Circle Line. At the time I can only remember being in an ecstasy of excitement about Jane joining the ship. Quite prepared to forgive Tom for the way he turned on me for speaking about Rosa, his girlfriend from home.

# Chapter 15

## Meeting Passengers and New Crew

We climbed the companionway accompanied by the rat a tat tat of a derrick being raised as the pawl hit against the ratchet. In the corridor leading to our cabins Tom, now calmed down, muttered that the ship was becoming like the flagship. He meant the refrigerated cargo liner carrying twelve passengers with such refinements as a marked out deck golf area, canopied for near all- weather play, plus swimming pool. A staff Captain to indulge the passengers plus their separate steward. A bronzed Adonis, invariably gay. A good practice environment for female passengers wanting to be flirtatious, knowing there was no likelihood of it going any further.

The Albany Princess was definitely down a grade or two from the flagship, but the passengers could still be high status. Other than meal times we were not expected to be in smart uniform. Tom said, changing into uniforms was a bit over the top, but there was a new Captain boarding and the First Mate probably wanted to make a good impression. 'What about caps?' I asked Tom. 'Wouldn't bother Mike,' was the reply. That all changed when we got to the top of the companionway and saw the First Mate in cap and uniform plus the Chief and Second steward also in uniform. The passengers were evidently going to get good attention.

'I can't take this,' said Tom. We're turning into P &O with uniform caps.' It was about turn back to our cabins—with Tom filching a clean cotton cap cover to replace the crumpled offering on his. White fitted plastic caps were mainly worn, but the black fabric cap with a white cotton cover plus company cap badge was considered both professional and traditional.

Our task was to assist the two new crew members, the Mate said. It was a scramble down the companionway. We were running late. I caught a glimpse of London style taxis further along the wharf—the drivers carrying cases towards a large pallet, with a roped net for securing the contents before being lifted on board by the derrick. Number Three hatch derricks were now raised in readiness. '—You two have just about made it,' said the Mate pointedly looking at his wrist watch. A deck hand was sugee-ing, vigorously along the bulkhead by the gangway. (Sugee-ing—Description: washing gloss painted accommodation with a cloth and bucket of hot soapy water, then cleaning off with fresh cold water) to wash the grimy paint work down—otherwise visible to the passengers as they boarded. The Mate wanted to have everything looking spick and span.

Two sailors were on the quay by the gangway. This normally open roped stairway was covered on both sides with strips of eyeleted green canvas, to reassure the passengers, I presume—that it was secure, but also for show. The company's flag was spread across the outside midway down the gangway. Red with an inner blue circle. The same as the funnel top. The Mate called out to the sailor to finish sugee-ing before turning to us. 'We'll walk along to meet the passengers. Miss Devlin will probably need assistance. She has a wheel chair and is accompanied by her brother.' We followed the Mate down The gangway past the cooling water outlet from the engine room, cascading partly into the dock, but also forming a puddle alongside the ship, before draining into the dock. The Mate addressed the two deck hands positioned at the foot of the gangway. 'You two may have to offer assistance to Miss Devlin, she has a wheel chair. The other passengers should have no problem climbing the gangway.' 'Do you mean a fireman's lift Mr Mate?' one sailor asked. Both sailors crossed their arms crouched and clasped each other's hands to signal prowess in this technique. This amused Tom and me—the Mate not at all. 'I'm hoping it won't come to that. I understand she can stand. It may just require assisting her out of the wheel chair and guiding her up the gangway. Anyway we'll cross that bridge when we get there.' He strode briskly towards the prow of the ship. Tom and I followed.

The white ship's name lettering was splashed with rust. 'That could be a job for you lads painting over those rust marks,' remarked the Mate 'Not at sea. Might be able to do it in Montevideo. Spruce up the look for Buenos Aires.' Tom raised his eyebrows giving me a sideways glance, as if to say does he never stop looking for jobs that need doing? It was to be fair, in the nature of First Mate's to be preoccupied with attending to the ship's appearance and the maintenance of deck equipment. The powerful stench of waxy compressed wool bales emanated from the warehouse, we were walking past. The passengers could be seen paying the cab drivers. Miss Devlin in her wheelchair, by the pallet of luggage.

The Mate waved to indicate they were not forgotten and that he was on the way across to where they were. We speeded up to keep up with the Mate's fast pace. 'Very pleased to welcome you all to Albany Princess. I'm the First Officer, Bert Thompson,' said the Mate. He proceeded to shake each of the passengers hands. After greeting Miss Devlin, who was a small dark haired lady in her fifties, wearing a beige duffel coat, gloves and scarf, he called Tom across. This young man will assist you to the gangway, if that's agreeable? 'But of course Mr Thompson. My brother will not mind someone pushing my chair. I'm a bit shaky on my pins when walking.' 'There are two sailors by the gangway to assist,' said the Mate. 'How thoughtful of you. I've climbed gangways before. I'm a bit slow, though. 'Slow and steady wins the race Miss Devlin. There's no hurry we're not sailing 'til tomorrow.' 'Oh I think I'll manage it by then Mr Thompson. Perhaps we'd better make a start,' she said turning and smiling at Tom now holding the handles at the back of the chair. Her brother chatting to Tom as they set off for the ship.

The two folk singers were removing large black guitar cases from the pallet. I went over to assist but they insisted on handling them by themselves. 'No, it is okay, we like to keep our guitars with us to be safe', said the dark, wiry man with a pencil thin moustache. The woman was slightly taller, with silver tasselled ear rings. She wore a pin striped suit, tossing her long black hair, expecting to be admired, while smiling with un-parted lips. Bright red lipstick and mascara black eyes contrasting with the grey of the docks. 'You can stay and guard the luggage lad,' the Mate said as he started back to the ship with the others.

It was as I stood by the pallet of luggage that I saw another taxi halted at the dock gates, getting permission to enter. The uniformed dock policeman pointing to the warehouses, which obscured the ship's hull and to where I was standing. I realized this was probably Captain and Mrs Anderson, and Jane and Christina arriving. Luggage was strapped to a flap at the back and also in the open access platform by the driver. When the taxi drew up I could only see Jane and Christina in the backseat. Jane stepped out nearest to me in a blue coat, scarf with matching leather gloves. Christina opened the opposite door. 'Surprised to see us again Mike?' she asked. I was scarcely able to contain myself on seeing Jane, but tried to make light of it. My rapid heart- beat betrayed my true feelings. 'I knew you two were joining the ship from Mr Thompson.' 'Whose Mr Thompson?' 'The First Mate. He told us your father's the new Captain. He said his daughter.' 'That's me,' said Jane. 'And a nurse friend,' I continued. '—Me!' Christina poked her head around from the other side of the taxi dressed similarly to Jane but in a dark green coat.—'Were, well, joining the ship as crew members.' 'And we thought, you two wouldn't've known,' said

Christina turning to Jane with a disappointed look. 'Where's Tom?' 'Oh, he's helping the passengers, up ahead,' I said trying to be nonchalant 'Do you want the luggage on here sir?' The taxi driver called out as he opened his door, pointing toward the pallet of luggage. This startled me, but then realizing he was addressing me. 'Yes,' driver I replied. The uniform and cap must have made him believe I was an officer. There were about six large suitcases, various grips and smaller cases. 'You're well prepared,' I said. 'It's not all ours most of it's my parents,' said Jane. A fine rain swept in from the dockside area making me want to get things moving. 'I'll just see what's happening by the gangway, a minute. Can you two keep an eye on the luggage?' The experience of them actually arriving, although being told about it, unbelievable.

Looking back I realized that I experienced that feeling of not wanting to be anywhere, but where I was. Living felt particularly agreeable at that moment. Although about to travel over five thousand miles the world I wanted to be in would be travelling with me. 'Will that be all young misses?' The taxi driver said placing the final case on to the pallet, no doubt waiting to be paid. I left Jane and Christina to settle the fare with the driver, and walked forward nearer to the quay-side to get a view of the gangway, obscured by the large corrugated warehouse.

First I saw the mooring ropes reaching to the sheer black bow of Albany Princess. Tom was walking back from assisting the passengers to board. I called out 'Tom, Tom, to attract his attention and walked towards him. 'Jane and Christina are here,' I called out. Tom quickened his pace. He appeared distracted. 'What's up? 'I asked. 'Those two singers, they just don't seem right.' The taxi was by the dock gates when I returned. Jane and Christina were sitting on a large black metal trunk. Christina seeing Tom waved. They'd been to the flicks together and seen more of each other. Both were relaxed about meeting again. They stood up as we approached. Tom kissed Christina on the lips with a 'Hi Chrissie,' and a 'great to see you.' He also gave Jane a kiss on the cheek. Nearly two years younger than Tom I lacked that kind of confidence with the opposite sex. The driver of the fork lift started it up, driving towards the pallet. 'Stand clear or the fork lift or it will pick you up,' I said 'How did you two get jobs on the ship?' Tom asked in a jokey manner, as if suggesting no one would want to employ them. 'That sounds as if it shouldn't be allowed Tom,' said Jane 'No I didn't mean that.' 'You're the nurse companion for the Devlin's, Christina,' I said, remembering the Mate mentioned this. 'How come you're working, when your father's the Captain?' asked Tom.

'That was my decision. I told Mike I'd like to work on a ship and the opportunity came when my father was offered the position as Captain. Is that a problem?' asked Jane. 'You could be like spying on us,' said Tom. 'Yes that's right the company has employed the two of us to spy on two teenage apprentices,' said Christina.

As senior apprentice I knew Tom would be keen to take charge. 'Follow me,' he said and we dutifully followed Tom along the dockside towards the gangway. At Number Three hatch the derrick was positioned over the side in preparation for loading the pallet of luggage. A sailor lent over the railing as the cargo hook descended signalling for the winch man to stop when it was about twelve feet above the dockside. Tom stood back to allow Christina and Jane to climb the gangway first.

Tom was just being Tom in questioning whether women should have a say about the world of work in what he considered a male sanctioned environment. The low level throb of the diesel generator, and blast from the engine room extract fans on the deck above greeted us as we walked towards the accommodation. The smell of baking bread caught in the breeze from the galley. Certainly preferable to the smells thrown up by ships discharge and the oily dockside. Jane and Christina went quiet, perhaps they were considering that the ship would be their home for the next three months.

'No more cooking Christina,' said Tom to Christina. 'You told me you hated cooking. You won't have to go shopping after work.' Christina looked pleased about that. Jane looked the most interested in the ship. 'When's Captain Anderson arriving?' I asked as we waited for Tom to open the door leading into the accommodation. 'They're at the shipping office. There's unrest in Argentina. I'm not supposed to say—hey you'd better promise not to tell I said that,' continued Jane. 'Don't worry, we stick together. Look after each other. It won't go any further,' I said. Tom stepped into the corridor holding back the door for Jane and Christina. 'When you said they, you mean?' 'My mother and father,' said Jane. 'That's going to be bit spooky,' said Tom. 'Having parents in the vicinity all the time. 'My dad's had to transfer to another ship, otherwise there would be three parents on board not just Jane's mum and dad,' 'Mine are old fashioned, but what parents aren't,' continued Jane.

The outer levers on the engine room door moved and it opened on to the corridor as we approached. The Fourth Engineer wiped his shoes on the inner mat before entering the corridor. 'Who have we got here then. Is this a guided tour?' he asked. 'No', said Tom. 'Jane, Christina meet Bill Mackay, Fourth engineer. They're joining the ship. Christina's a nurse and Jane's working her passage on deck.'

'If you ever get bored you can always help out in the engine room love,' he said to Jane. 'I won't shake hands we're working on a generator. Don't take any cheek from those two, they're full of the old blarney, but I can see you look far too sensible for that.'

# Chapter 16

# Settling In

Wann walked down the corridor towards us as Bill went into the Mess Room. 'If you please to follow me. Chief Steward tell Wann to make self useful and show Miss Jane and Miss Christina to their cabins. My name Is Wann.' 'I'm Jane,' and 'I'm Christina,' they said in reply. 'Miss Jane, Miss Christina. Wann much happy to welcome you aboard.' He gave a bow to first Jane and then Christina before shaking hands. 'Wann to show you to your cabins. If you follow please, when ready?' A pause followed before Jane said, 'We're ready.' 'Yes,' said Christina. Both smiled back at Wann. 'It is this way please,' he said walking past us toward the companionway. 'See you in a bit,' said Tom as they followed Wann along the corridor.

I joined Tom in his cabin. 'It's great that we've already met,' Away from the ship. I really fancy Jane now. Those legs—couldn't keep my eyes off them when she walked up the gang-way. Tom having followed Jane, with me behind Tom. 'Don't know how I missed them at the dance.' 'Perhaps, because you were with Christina most of the time,' I said. It was not some-thing that escaped my notice. It was like a re-run of nights ashore with Tom, where he got the pick of a pair of girls, often because he was that bit older. Now he seemed to be show-ing a preference for Jane. 'They're going to have the other two passenger cabins,' he said. 'You didn't expect them to be in cabins in the crews quarters, did you?' I said sprawled on his day bed.

Although Tom had taken Christina to the pictures and obviously got on with her, there seemed a distinct possibil-ity he'd be giving Jane more attention. Jane was friendly with me, but I was seventeen to her twenty two I was at an early stage of learning the lessons of love, empathising with the Buddy Holly song, which I felt might be applicable to my situation.

Mr Thompson's figure framed the doorway and I removed my legs from the day bed to the floor. 'There's some hand luggage to be taken to the cabins. One can fetch this from the deck. The other can show the young women around the accommodation area.' 'I'll show them around Chief,' said Tom straightaway. 'I don't mind which one of you does. I don't want Captain and Mrs Anderson saying their daughter's not welcome aboard.' Mr Thompson not then knowing we'd already met Jane and Christina. Another First Mate might have then kept us apart. On my first trip we saw Mr Thompson in the Jousten Hotel, Buenos Aires having a meal with a younger woman. I was with Tom prior to being shown Buenos Aires at night. We were in the half section with just plain wooden tables and chairs. Mr Thompson and girlfriend in the white table clothed area by a window with flowers on the table. Two white coated waiters danced attendance. The staff believed to be some of the crew from the Graf Spee, scuttled in the River Plate during World War Two. It was an efficiently run establishment.

When we reported for work duties next day Tom questioned Mr Thompson with, 'Was the meal at the Jousten up to standard last night, sir? His face reddened before he replied. 'Yes,—and there was I believing the world was out of sight—Tom Blake.' 'I might as well tell you that I'm getting married to Juliana,' he said, perhaps concerned we might put another interpretation on the liaison. 'Congratulations sir,' Tom said. 'Yes, 'I said a bit taken aback by Tom's inquisitiveness. 'I can't remember that much about the meal, matter of fact. Only that she said yes to becoming engaged. There's no need to make it public knowledge though.' We gave each other a look of surprise. 'Course not Chief,' said Tom. Will she come back on the ship?' 'Hold on,' said the Mate. 'We got engaged, not married.'

'Who'd of thought the old goat had it in him,' said Tom afterwards. Amazingly we both kept it a secret from the crew. It perhaps explained why Mr Thompson was in a happy frame of mind knowing he was meeting up with Juliana in three weeks. Tom excused any disagreeable schedules given to us by the Mate with the words '—but he's in luve.' There was scant chance of Jane not being made welcome on board, but you learn as an apprentice that Mate's have foibles and fussiness about all manner of things.

After Mr Thomson left I made my way to the main deck. Angelo was standing in the chalked area guarding two suit-cases. He looked relieved to see me. 'Hello Mike, you are here for the suitcases. I can go for my dinner now, that is good.' They were both heavy. With one in each hand they were not dissimilar to the solid weight of derrick head blocks. I staggered to the companionway and carried one up at a time. Repeating the procedure with each companionway. I bumped into the Second Steward on reaching the passenger deck level. 'Where are the two young women crew they need to collect their bed linen from the laundry locker?' he said, as I stopped outside the cabin doors numbered three and four. 'They're with Tom.' The Second opened the cabin doors with separate keys and I placed the luggage in number three cabin. It looked out on to the funnel deck. I could see through the porthole Tom describing the finer points of the davit launching system on the lifeboat. I turned to the Second. 'They're out on deck. They look as if they might welcome a break from the techni-cal tour of the ship.' He went out on deck. I caught up with Tom left standing by the lifeboat. 'You did tell them dinner is at eighteen thirty?' I asked. 'I did, Mike. They're coming down at twenty past.'

The main luggage was being carried across the Boat Deck

by two sailors with Wann directing more than carrying. 'Bit of useful muscle power,' said Tom. Wann the steward was short and skinny. 'Will Wann be the passengers steward?' 'I imagine so,' said Tom. 'Not the usual type of passenger steward.' Tom speaking from his vast experience of serving on one of the company's more passenger orientated liners. It was six o'clock and we were already in uniform. 'It just seems such an unlikely situation,' said Tom, as I returned to sprawling on the day bed in his cabin. 'That we should meet them at that dance. I took Christina to the flicks, but we didn't arrange to keep in touch, and she knew the ship would be away for three months.' 'If you believe in fate then it wasn't a coincidence, now that they're on board.' 'It's probably a sort of family trip with Jane's mother being born in Rosario,' I said, looking at Tom's full length poster of Petula Clark on his wall, thinking that Christina's hair was very similar in length. 'You never told me that Mike,' said Tom turning to look at me, while blowing cigarette smoke from his mouth and nose, eyes narrowed, but not just from the smoke, into a critical look. The furrowed forehead, and raised eyebrows said,—'What's your explanation for not telling me about this then?' 'You said yourself in the dry dock that our chances of meeting them were slim to non-existent, so I never thought to mention it,' I said. Which was true.

Captain Anderson's wife is almost bound to know my family. It's not that big a town. 'Jane said her mother's family have an estancia.' 'I can't see how you never thought to tell me this—Mike?' I went on leave and I probably would have got round to telling you, but then you said in the dry dock we'd probably never see them again. I didn't see it as important'. Tom calmed down, perhaps realizing that it was in fact just as I said. 'And 'I said, 'then there's Rosa.' Tom pointed a finger at me as a warning not to continue, but I did. 'You told me you're all but engaged. You're going to have to tell Christina about Rosa.' I admit I was trying to stir things now that Tom was showing an interest in Jane. 'No, of course I didn't. Rosa may not hang around. You know what it's like, they're all over you while you're there, knowing that you won't be in port that long.' 'No, Tom,' I said, 'you've known Rosa since you were a child living next door. It's not quite like that. Are you complaining about their being on board? That it might cramp your style in Montevideo or Buenos Aires,' I asked Tom. 'No, it's great they're on board, but—but it's not like being ashore. You're working and their working and then Jane dad's the Captain.' 'When I spoke to Jane she was keen on the idea of working on board a ship like this. I don't think she'll expect favours, because her dad's the Captain. Probably the opposite.'

Just then I heard Jane and Christina's voices and the Second Engineer introducing himself to them. 'Your father's not with us this trip, then,' he said. 'We were going to travel together, but a week before dad received a cable. Apparently a ship docked with engine problems,' said Christina. 'And your father is the expert, you needn't explain. It's the Imperial Shipper. It's happened before and no one else can sort it.' 'You already know about it?' 'No, but when you said a ship with engine problems. Your father's the expert. The problem is he hasn't been replaced and it's near to sailing.' 'I was looking forward to him being on board,' said Christina. 'Welcome aboard to the both of you, anyway,' said the Second Engineer.

'You liar, 'I heard Jane say as they came along the corridor. 'You said you were glad that both our fathers weren't on board.' 'I've never needed smart clothes to eat in the evening, even in a restaurant,' said Christina, just as they arrived outside Tom's cabin door. 'This isn't a restaurant this is a cargo liner,' Jane replied. The cabin door was wide open and her hand reached in to knock on the door. 'Are women crew allowed in or is this just for male apprentices?'

A gong started sounding outside the dining saloon, which was about twenty five feet from Tom's cabin. That would be Wann by the saloon door banging the gong. 'Shove up Mike there's room for three on the day bed,' said Tom. Jane was wearing a dark blue skirted suit, which looked great and Christina was in a green dress with puffed sleeves and a large coloured stone necklace that reached nearly to waist level. They must have noticed us having our eyes out on storks in appreciation. 'We've been given instructions to dress smart for meals. Christina says she'll be putting in for a clothing allowance,' said Jane. 'No I was only joking. It's worth it when you don't have to cook meals in a flat any longer,' said Christina. 'Christina can't get over getting dressing up and then being waited on.' 'Yes,' said Tom the food on merchant ships is usually good. The Mate says he's well fed, but poorly paid. I don't know where that places us, earning less than a deck boy. 'Well fed maintenance workers?' I suggested.

'The Chief has said you're to sit on the long table with us two and the engineers. There's never usually a room full of people, because watch keeping means some are sleeping or on watch. Captain Anderson hasn't arrived yet.' 'No they're at the agent's office. We've been sent on ahead,' said Jane. 'Oh, I was forgetting, I'll have to be careful what I say.' 'Yes I'll be writing in my diary everything you two say and then give it to my father, so he can straighten you out later,' said Jane. 'I'll think I'll do the same,' said Christina. A sort of medical record.' Tom realized he was being taken for a ride and shut up.

Jane and Christina were sat near enough to see Tom's full length poster of Petula Clark. 'I never realized she was so flat chested,' said Christina, turning to Jane. It was not something I'd given consideration to. Anyway that dream girl appreciation I might have held for the pop singer was fast vanishing now that Jane was on board Albany Princess. It was as well the wardrobe door was closed. There were pictures of naked women in compromising positions. Tom obtained these from the Chief Steward to decorate his wardrobe. I didn't suggest there were more voluptuous example of womanhood pinned on the inside of the door. Already I was beginning to realize this trip was going to be different. I didn't then anticipate how different though.

# Chapter 17

# Meeting Up with the Fifth Engineer

I came out of my semi-dream state when Wann banged the gong for a final call. 'I'll have to get my Jacket, from next door,' I said. Tom's chair was turned around facing the day bed. As I stood up he pulled his chair back, both Jane and Christina moved their legs to one side to let me through. On returning from my cabin Tom was leading Jane and Christina along the corridor towards the Dining Saloon. I followed, while Tom stopped outside the door to let them in first, directing them to the long table, which ran towards the kitchen galley hatch. The two round tables opposite—next to the windows, over-looked the after deck and were for senior officers and passengers. The large corner one which faced the door we entered by, being Captain Anderson's, which would now seat his wife the four passengers, and the First Mate.

The Fifth Engineer got up, placed his serviette on the table in front of him, before walking around the table to introduce himself. 'Hello I'm Andrew Staples. Are you just visiting? You're welcome to sit anywhere you like. Everyone seems to be ashore.' Jane's face reddened. The Fifth was twenty four with brown hair. His face still a nut brown from the last trip. 'No we're working on board, said Jane. We've just arrived.'

Wann expertly held open the galley door with his right foot and knee whilst carrying a steaming plate of food and bowl of vegetables , swivelled around—kicked the door further open with his foot, before calling out. 'Miss Jane, Miss Christina, perhaps you would like to sit opposite each other next to Mr Tom and Mr Mike. No doubt, following instructions given by the Chief Steward, previously. The Fifth returned to his seat before Wann arrived with the meal. I could see he was working his charm, both Jane and Christina were blushing from the attention. The Fifth was the resident Don Juan. There was a sultry beauty in Montevideo who would be waiting for Andrew on the dock as the ship tied up. In Buenos Aires a blond bombshell of German extraction. In Rosario a very pretty Roman Catholic school teacher, fully aware the male population lusted after her, but unlikely to succumb. Tom his relationship expert cap on, had decided that she intended marrying the Fifth, after he complained she never let her guard down and only permitted kissing. That she was not a pushover.

'Have you been to Buenos Aires?' The Fifth turned towards where Jane and Christina were sitting, a chair separating him from Christina. 'No , I've only been on the Irish ferry before,' she said. 'I'm travelling as sort of nurse and carer to a passenger.' 'A nurse. That's a very useful occupation. You do realize you'll be having crew members wanting you to treat their sun burn. The Chief Steward will no longer be required in his medical role. Are you Jane or Christina?' 'Christina.' Christina turned away to talk to Jane. Tom's face a picture of annoyance, following Andrew's long conversation with her. Wann held the menu in front of Christina and she asked for fish kedgeree as did Jane. After the main course arrived Andrew, got up to leave. 'I'd like to stop and talk, but I'm on watch in ten minutes,' he said.

Tom looked relieved, turning to Jane and Christina. 'How are you two feeling?' 'How do you mean? How are we feeling?' replied Christina 'Not feeling seasick then?' 'We're still in port, how can we feel seasick?' 'It's been known to happen.' 'You're making that up,' said Christina. I interrupted Tom's banter. 'We'd better get a move on. We're supposed to be taking you to meet Mr Thompson, the First Mate, straight after the meal.'

# Chapter 18

# Instructions for All Four

'Welcome aboard Miss Anderson and Christina Wilkins is that right?' The Mate greeted Jane and Christina, standing up from where he was working on the Rolston in the middle of the wheelhouse. He shook hands with them. Tom and myself followed behind into the wheelhouse from the windswept bridge. 'Welcome aboard Albany Princess. We'll soon be leaving all this wind, rain and winter behind. Well in a few days, anyway. I hope these two lads have been looking after you. Showing you around.' We stood by the rolled open bridge door.

'Come in and close that door you two. I'm Mr Thompson the First Mate as I'm sure you already know. I hesitate to even guess what these two have said about me, but I'm the one who has to account for safe cargo stowage. Not only the cargo'— he swept his hand past the Rolston with its mahogany box and shiny brass weights, out towards the deck spread beneath the wheelhouse windows. 'But also the deck crew and overall good practice.' Jane looked intrigued by the situation of meeting Mr Thompson and the general layout of the wheelhouse.... her eyes wide open with a look of attentiveness across her face. Christina's showed understanding with a look of familiarity. Afterwards, she said that the Mate reminded her of the matron at the hospital. I did not say that the Mate may be referred to as 'the old woman' complementing the Captain's name of 'the old man.' 'There are ground rules, continued the Mate. Miss Wilkins you are a nurse and should be expected to be addressed as Nurse Wilkins, by the crew. Miss Anderson similarly formalities will be maintained. This is probably just common sense to you, but to keep the right balance on board it is to be understood that you must be respectful of the crew and they will be expected to do likewise. No entering the crews quarters for you two. There should in everyday circumstances be no reason for this to occur. I have my spies everywhere'— the Mate, glanced in our direction and smiled as he continued talking. 'Similarly you two lads, that visit to the passengers quarters with the luggage is the only visit required.'

'We've met Miss Anderson and Miss Wilkins before sir,' said Tom. 'Where was this?' The Mate looked puzzled. 'At a disco dance, when we docked in Liverpool.' 'Are you two sure you want to stay on board?' The Mate glanced first at Jane then Christina, impassively, before looking forward from the wheel- house on to the hatches below. There was a silence, before he continued, first turning to look at us. 'This wouldn't have happened in my day'—but he smiled. 'Are you expecting disco dancing on board? You didn't arrange for the folk singers to come along to provide backing to continue the dancing, I suppose?' 'It was Saturday night at the Electric Hall. Just a chance meeting,' said Tom. 'We were saying earlier,' Tom looked at me for back up. 'We never expected to meet Christina—I mean Nurse Wilkins and Miss Anderson again.' 'Don't give too much away lad. Christina never short of a quick remark, said, 'It was a surprise to us Mr Thompson, but we're getting over it, aren't we Jane?' 'Yes,' Jane said conspiratorially.

Voices could be heard as the chart room door opened. The Mate left us in the wheelhouse, and walked across. 'Hello Bert,' a woman's voice spoke first. 'Would it be all right for Jane and Christina to join us? 'They might be working.' I heard Captain Anderson's deeper voice join in. Captain and Mrs Anderson must have boarded while we'd been talking to the Mate. 'I don't expect special treatment for my daughter. They both'll need to pull their weight.' Christina raised her hand pointing a finger at Jane, before realizing she was being included in the instructions. 'I've a few things to give them Paul, that's all,' said Mrs Anderson. Jane's father as Captain, was in charge, but the reality of the situation was that neither Jane nor Christina could be seen to be having special treatment as crew members. 'That's perfectly all right Mrs Anderson,' said the Mate. 'I've been laying down some ground rules, whilst on board—that's fine by me.'

The four of us were standing looking out of the wheelhouse windows watching the crew replacing railings next to the hatches after the Mate went across to the chartroom. At number two hatch Chippy was having the tarpaulins covering the hatches pulled back by crew members. A fresh new wooden hatch was leant up against the hold—the galvanised metalled end more silvery than the old hatch it was to replace.

The old one looked splintered halfway down when lifted out. The Mate probably spotted this giving replacement instructions to Chippy. It was anybody's guess as to what mistreatment the stevedore's inflicted on it. The three crew members were not overly keen, since while the Mate was giving his talk to us they covered the hatch and lifted the locking bars into place. Then Chippy arrived gripping the hatch by the metal hand hold, with the deck boy at the other end. The sailors not best pleased at having to remove the locking bars and tarpaulins.

Jane and Christina were between the two of us watching proceedings on deck. Tom's face broke into a smile as he watched the crew swearing about having to remove the tarpaulins, but the mutterings ceased when the Bosun arrived and took charge of the situation. For myself and Tom this was a classic—watching Chippy getting into an altercation with the crew. They quickly went from resenting Chippy disturbing their work to showing diligence once the Bosun arrived.

It was lost on Jane and Christina whose eyes were glued watching two Deck Hands further up on the hatch—one of whom did a walking handstand across the tarpaulin before back flipping on to the deck. I saw the Bosun raise his hand and finger point as he reprimanded him for this. Jane and Christina clapped at the acrobatics, although out of sight and sound. 'Ah,' said the Mate, returning from the chart room, 'I've been waiting for Chippy to replace that hatch.' 'Miss Anderson your mother requested you be called Miss Taylor,' said the Mate. 'Oh, yes, apparently I'm to work incommunicado,' said Jane. 'I didn't know your parents were that ashamed of you,' said Christina. 'No it's about keeping it secret from the crew, apparently,' said Jane. 'Heavens knows why.' 'Well your mother would like to see both of you' said the Mate.

A dark haired woman with greying hair stepped out from behind the chart room door, smiling at the group of us. Jane and Christina walked across. The Mate grabbed the megaphone and went to the side of the bridge.

'Make sure that old hatch is destroyed Chips.' The Mate's magnified voice breaking the evening's quiet. 'Aye, Aye Mr Mate I'll be seeing to that. I've already marked it condemned,' pointing to a chalked circle with a cross, he called back from the deck below.

'We're sailing, as soon as the pilot boards, at first light,' said the Mate entering the wheelhouse. 'Expect an early call.'

# Chapter 19

# New Third Engineer

I stood behind the wheel at eight fifteen, only to be sent below by the Third Mate. 'Assistance with a crew member's luggage is needed by the gangway,' he said in a superior manner, before disappearing into the chart room like some high ranking official. When I stepped out on to the embarkation deck Tom was there 'You took your time,' he said, as if I'd taken a break on my way down from the bridge. The crew member, in a dark overcoat held an initialled suitcase. He smiled. Even at this first meeting I got a sense that this was someone attempting to blend into a new role. Tall with an assurance of a person, capable of leading more than being led. 'Good of you two to give us a hand,' he said, before taking a final draught on his cigarette, kneeling down to stub it out in the sand of a fire bucket.

'That's all right, welcome aboard,' I responded. 'Fraid it's a little on the heavy side, 'he pointed to a black tin trunk at the foot of the gangway left standing upright on a sack truck. 'Two of us should be able to manage. Your cabin's down the corridor from us, next deck up,' said Tom 'Who is he Tom?' I asked as our feet rattled gangway rungs down to the dock. 'The new Third Engineer.' 'A replacement for Christina's dad?—Mr Watkins.' 'Yes, how d'you know that?' he shouted up to the Second Mate at the stern. 'He said he was the replacement Third and could someone give a hand with his case. The Second buzzed the bridge to get you down to help me.'

A figure in scarf, car coat and kid gloves arrived at the gangway, and removed what looked like a pass from his coat pocket as we lifted the tin box. 'Cutting that a bit fine,' he said, as he jumped on to the gangway. The peep of first one tug arriving and then another made me realize he must be the pilot. I felt the metal handle of the box cutting into my hand as we reached deck level. The Bosun, was leaning over the railings. 'Leave that there for the stewards. You two need to be at your stations.' The new arrival turned to us as we placed his trunk on the deck. 'Thanks for that I know the layout of the ship. You'd best do as the Bosun says.'

There was a whirring sound as the hoist began hauling the gangway up from the dock for stowing. Tom returned to assist the Second Mate at the stern and I went back to the wheelhouse. I was on the wheel until the ship left the dock basin,—the eight to twelve watch then took over. My next watch came around too fast. The first hour of look out was a running commentary on light sightings. The Monkey island above the wheelhouse, a modern equivalent of the Crow's Nest, meant as lookout you saw masthead lights early.

The lights of Liverpool faded as we left on a course of 261 degrees until the ship was clear of the North Wales coastline and into the Irish Sea when there was a sharp swing to port and on to 201 degrees. 'Light fifty degrees on starboard bow,' I called down the voice pipe alerting the bridge to train binoculars on the light. It was a clear night. Frequent reporting of ship's lights, meant the hour passed quickly. The Mate on occasion made starboard alterations of course to avoid approaching North bound traffic.

I assisted the Mate in taking bearings, after finishing the lookout duty. By steering 198 degrees and getting positions from the Decca Navigator at ten minute intervals, the ship crawled back to the course line of 201, following repeated earlier alterations to avoid oncoming ships.

Motor Vessel Albany Princess carved her way through the sea with a rolling motion. It was better being on the wheel, than standing on the Monkey island, togged up to keep out the cold. I was on the wheel from seven to eight, by which time the ship was distancing from the coast on a Great circle course which would take us to the Cape Verde Islands for re-fuelling in about seven days.

There was no moon light to lick across the sea and give shadowy vision, of hatches and foredeck as I made small repeated adjustments to keep on course. The Mate's cigarette no longer glowing red was the real indication that the day was taking over from night. It was seven thirty when I glanced at my watch—the minute hand appeared stopped by forces holding back time itself, leading to that trapped feeling of perhaps having to steer the ship forever—deep into eternity. 'Good morning Mr Mate it's good to be under way again sir, isn't it?' Chips entered the wheelhouse to my left. He allowed his smile to pan across to where I was standing, removing his battered trilby when the Mate replied. 'Good morning Chips.'

'Two new crew members this trip Mr Mate. Two young women. Company for the young apprentices, perhaps? 'They are crew members Chippy no different from anyone else.' The Mate lowering the binoculars from his eyes before continuing. 'Well that's not quite true. The fair haired girl is the Captain's daughter.' 'Really, is that so Mr Mate,' exclaimed Chips. I could see from his surprised look, that he genuinely did not know. 'Yes. It has been decided,' said the Mate, 'that the crew are not to be informed of the relationship. The information is that she's visiting her mother in Buenos Aires. Captain Anderson and Mrs Anderson decided that it is better that the crew are not told about the relationship. That she blends in as a crew member. You, the Bosun and officers will be aware of the situation, but not the lower deck and boiler room ratings.' I wasn't at the time convinced that this could be affected , without it leaking out that Jane was actually Captain Anderson's daughter. 'I understand Mr Mate. I will tell no one,' said Chips, turning to me and saying, 'You boys understand this?' I nodded my head in agreement 'Yes. She is called Miss Jane Taylor, when anyone asks.' 'I completely understand Mr Mate,' said Chips. Although I wasn't convinced Chippie Angelo would be able to contain himself from gossiping, but he sounded convincing. 'I will tell no one, nor should you,' he said again turning towards me. 'Miss Taylor will work with the apprentices, but there is the new flag locker that I want you to complete on the monkey island, Chips. In the afternoons she will assist you with this when we get to warmer latitudes.'

The Mate took hold of the binoculars placed on the ledge by the wheelhouse windows, pushed his glasses to his forehead and scanned the horizon from left to right. He retraced a second time to look at a passenger liner that was rapidly overhauling us on the port side. Angelo, stood in front of me his hunched pixie like figure relaxed, over long arms at his side. The Mate, binoculars still glued to eyes, asked, 'How are you progressing with the wedging of the hatches?' Chippie clasped hands together, eyes lighting like a man discovering treasure. 'Mr Mate I've prepared the bags of wedges ready by the mastheads. 'That's good Chips,' replied the Mate replacing the binoculars in their holster. 'After breakfast the apprentices and Miss Taylor can assist you with securing them in place,' said the Mate.

'I will then be on the foredeck, Mr Mate. Is that all for now Mr Mate, sir? 'Yes Chips, but there is fresh timber, which needs preparing for shifting boards and hatches. I will talk with you tomorrow.' 'Thank you Mr Mate, it is so good of you to give me your time sir, if that is all for now Mr Mate.' 'Yes Chips, that is all.'

It was Mr Mate this and Mr Mate that. Even "Mr Chief Mate, sir", from Angelo. An obsequiousness that could be perceived as irritating, but not it appeared to Mr Thompson. Angelo worked as a shipwright assisting to build Mussolini's navy during the Second World War. He was proud of this and the Mate valued his expertise, but he would have done better not to ever mention his wartime experiences to the crew. He was friendly and helpful to both of us apprentices, and highly skilled in his work. He missed his Welsh wife and on occasion used to go on conversational excursions about his life with her—with details, beyond the need to know level.

# Chapter 20

# The Bosun Given Work Assignment

Ronan Kelly, the Bosun looked into the Wheelhouse, hoping to catch the Mate's eye. He wore a black trilby, cream woollen shirt black crossed pattern, sleeves buttoned at the wrist and a leather waistcoat—a gold chain dangling from one pocket concealing a fob watch. He walked back across the deck and leant on the mahogany rail that ran beneath the green painted windbreak. Ronan Kelly I felt was wary of Angelo. He walked on deck with a rolling gait, which could be exaggerated with his being partial to a few beers accompanied with a rum chaser. In fairness at sea, he managed to maintain a reasonably coherent grasp on his responsibilities, but in port less so. Angelo would warn of the demon drink, and remark on how the Bosun was caught in its grasp. Ronan probably worried that Angelo might report him to the Mate on his bridge visits and this meant there could be a tense atmosphere between the two.

'Top of the morning to you, sir,' called out the Bosun, as Angelo left the wheelhouse by the opposite door. He stepped over the brass floor runner and into the wheelhouse. 'Good morning to you Bosun.' 'It's good to be away from the dirt and smoke and to be back at sea, to be sure,' said the Bosun. 'Yes, we look forward to reaching port Bosun, but dockside becomes tedious after a time,' replied Mr Thompson. 'There's a big task ahead of us Bosun. The company has given instructions for the accommodation housing to be repainted. This will mean stripping the paint away and red leading before we reach Montevideo. This shouldn't interfere with the progress of over hauling derrick blocks and the replacing and greasing of running wires.' 'Ah the lads will not be without work then this trip,' said the Bosun.

I glanced again at my watch, relieved to see it was now ten to eight. I heard the chart room door from the accommodation open and close. The Third Mate entered the wheelhouse. 'One minute Bosun I'll just hand the watch over to the Third.' He left the Bosun standing in the corner of the Wheelhouse. 'There's a passenger ship overhauling us, but nothing up ahead. We're clear of the main shipping lanes around the coast,' he said to the Third. 'The course is 201 degrees. You'll have seen the chart. It's dead reckoning until we get a midday position. There's a lookout. I should clear it with Captain Anderson, before you do away with the lookout or go on to automatic pilot. He'll almost certainly be on the bridge before breakfast.'

Mr Thomson walked back into the chart room, no doubt to affirm with the Third the ship's position, as anticipated and also to write up the ship's log. This was a comment on the weather usually and hopefully not some dire event that occurred during the watch, that needed recording, like a fire on board. A few minutes passed while the watch was officially handed over by the Mate. The Third looked at the radar and then went out on to the bridge to locate the passenger ship, which was now well ahead of us. There was nothing visible that required watching or likely to need a course alteration according to the Mate, and the Third seemed happy to takeover.

The discussion about how the crew were to be deployed continued with the Bosun on the portside of the bridge. The relief wheelman arrived and that meant the four to eight watch was over for me as well. I noticed that the ship was pitching and rolling more significantly than when I went on watch. We were away from the coast and into the more exposed waters of the Atlantic.

Tom was full of himself, after returning from the dining saloon. I was standing outside his cabin door, while he sat on his daybed lighted cigarette in hand. 'They left in a hurry half way through breakfast.' 'Who did?' I asked. 'Two of the passengers with Jane and Christina,' he continued. 'I don't see why that makes you happy, just because the motion of the ship never affects you.' Tom was amused when I was sea sick on my first trip. I got over it, but met with ribbing and ridicule from Tom 'By the way,' I said, 'You do know we're lined up for assisting Chips with the hatch wedging, and Jane as well.' 'Don't expect she'll be up to it.'

Just as I opened my cabin door the Mate stopped outside Tom's cabin and I heard him tell him about working with Chippy and that Jane would be joining us. I changed into my uniform and made for the dining saloon. The Mate would expect us out on deck before him. He did not linger over breakfast.

# Chapter 21

# Wedging on Deck

We met Wann in the corridor as we prepared to leave for the foredeck. 'Miss Jane tell me not to say she is fighting fit, but she's coming to work. She come down now soon.' 'Tell Miss Taylor Wann we'll be outside,' said Tom, 'just the other side of the door,' who usually started the day with a cigarette on the corridor deck outside our cabins. 'When Miss Jane arrives I see from saloon,—okayee I say where you are hiding.' 'We're not hiding Wann.'

Fortunately Jane stepped into the corridor avoiding Tom getting irate with Wann for skewing the meaning. 'Feeling better?' I asked. 'Yes—thanks for asking Mike. The fresh air will probably help.' Breakfast smells like bacon, toast and cigarette smoke mixed into the air conditioning in the corridor making it unpleasant, without the motion of the ship, for anyone with sea sickness. Jane in a boiler suit and bobble hat, looked attractive in the way good looking women often do when dressed in clothing more often worn by men.

I thought she was brave to not let seasickness get her down. Occasional spray in the breeze was enervating as we stepped on to the main deck from the accommodation. Angelo not much taller than the hatches wearing a black woollen hat and faded blue jacket was standing hammering wedges into the cleats by Number One Hatch. We kept to the dry middle—walking to the foredeck. We gathered around Chippy.

'You see the longer edge goes against the cleat. Those up here at the front of the hatch go with the wedge's skinny part pointing aft. Like so.' Chippy pulled wedge out of the burlap sack placing it in the cleat and hammering it into position.

'May I call you Jane? Although we're supposed to call you

Miss Taylor,' he asked Jane. 'Yes that's all right. You don't mind being called Angelo do you?' said Jane. 'That is very fair of you to say. We're going to get on champion I can see.'

'You boys know the score. All wedges need to place in cleats. At end of hatch they go other way. The waves on deck, you see, ride forward and hit them in reverse direction.' A spurt of sea water whipped across the railings by Number Two hatch smacking on to the deck and hatch. 'We'd better get a-moving, the waves they start break on board, more. You apprentices can work together. Place wedges in Numbers Two and Three hatch. Jane will stay with me and help wedge—rest of Number One. I able to check, they right as go by. Not be long on foredeck.'

This was familiar to me from the other times on leaving port—the wedges, a final security measure to ensure the tarpaulins were secure on the hatches. We might later have to assist in the 'tween decks where cargo was wired into position. Chippy would cast an expert eye over lashing down and cargo protection—single decker buses and lorry chassis, for example. The Mate perhaps unhappy with the stowage of one or two items, may already have directed Chippy to put extra dunnage in place or additional ties. A test for the safe stowage of cargo could come suddenly. Weather deteriorating, waves building, followed by pitching and pounding of the bow could place strain on wires attached to pillars, beams and bulkheads. A bus breaking loose in a 'tween deck and then thrown into the lower hold would not only inflict damage on other cargo, but could lead to upsetting the ship's stability. It was not unknown for a ship to return to port after cargo became dislodged at the outset in heavy seas.

We would shortly be crossing the Bay of Biscay, where invariably rougher waters were met. Sudden falls from the continental shelving plus distorted configuration on the sea bed were suspects, for vigorous wave making. Tom and I took turns carrying the sack of wedges while the other pushed a wedge into the cleat. We made trips for additional bags of wedges from the mast housing—substantial welded structures, constructed around the mast. Both mast and housing having to support heavy lifting derricks. The mast house was a locker room with door access to the ladders leading first down to the 'tween decks and then the lower holds. On completion we returned to where Jane and Chippy were standing behind the mast housing. A wave sprayed on to the side of the housing as further instructions were given. 'There are wedges in the after housing. It is best I finish now. You three continue wedging Number Four and Five hatches.' We left Chippy dancing from wedge to wedge, deftly hitting the hammer on each protruding wedge. One skilled bash seating the wedge against the metal baton beneath.

'Will he be all right?' asked Jane as we walked aft, and into the relative shelter of the accommodation. 'It's not too bad, yet. He'll not get washed overboard if that's what you think,' said Tom. 'Angelo would be off that deck, if he thought it was too risky. He's okay.' It didn't occur to me that there was risk involved, but then Jane was now the novice like I was on my first trip, still finding her sea legs. Not so confident about being on the main deck at sea.

We met the Bosun, who was supervising the suggee-ing around the accommodation housing. 'How's the little devil? You haven't left him to the mercy of the waves have ye now?' He said, mischievously. Jane wasn't sure how to take this and looked at me in a quizzical sort of way. The Bosun would joke about Angelo. 'Don't worry he doesn't mean anything. He's a bit of a jester,' I said. But out of earshot of Jane, Tom said to me, 'I'm not so sure.'

The wind funnelled through the corridor, but as we emerged from the accommodation it was like another country on the after deck. 'It's so calm here you wouldn't believe there're waves breaking on the foredeck,' said Jane. There was more vibration, due to engine proximity with thrust from the prop shaft beneath deck. The stern was rising and sinking in the moderate sea. The sound of the Doxford engine escaped from the funnel, fluctuating as the ship moved forward, whilst surging up and down in response to the head sea.

# Chapter 22

# First Port Montevideo

My first work assignment with Jane, without Tom was painting out the Tally Clerk's Locker so that it was fresh and clean. We roller brushed the deck head and bulkheads with white paint, taking It in turns to get a breath of air while the other continued painting, when the fumes built up. Jane was keen like me to get work outside once we were away from the winter weather. We were detailed off for paint chipping and scraping in the days that followed. Albany Princess was in the tropics when Jane, said. 'Look at those,' calling back to me as she stepped on to the upper deck. The ship surged upwards causing pressure on our feet and legs in the Atlantic rollers. 'They've actually got wings that spread from their sides,' she said pulling open the wing of a plump flying fish that had collided with the railing and landed on the deck during the night. They reminded me of mackerel jumping from the sea to evade predators. Jane threw it back overboard. 'Hey a sailor would have cut of the wings sliced it open and grilled it,' I said. 'They're not that desperate for food are they?' 'No but they're tasty,' I said.

We grabbed the railing running along the accommodation to steady ourselves. Both holding, in one hand, a large paint tin with scraper, chipping hammer and wire brush. The other hand free to hold on with. One hand for the ship one for yourself, as the Mate was apt to say. It was a three week voyage for a ship like Albany Princess to Buenos Aires. Best speed about fourteen and knots. The passenger liners knocked several days off this figure. With powerful steam turbines able to adjust speed for arrival on a specific day and tide—weather permitting.

Two days ago this side of the ship reeked with the smell of diesel from the small tanker that came alongside at the Cape Verde Islands when we lay at anchor. Oil pumped into tanks for the round trip. It was over a fortnight to go before we reached Montevideo, but now shirt sleeve weather. Deck hands dispensed with shirts, and resorted to cut away jeans, but risked getting sunburned and unable to work. This was termed self- inflicted and they could be fined a day's pay. The past two days had been spent scraping and chipping paint from the railings and housing in the accommodation area.

Tom now on the 12-4 watch ostensibly to assist the Second Mate with Notices to Mariners chart updates. There was a metal gully underneath the railings, where I was working, which was badly rusted. With my left hand holding the middle rail I chipped away at the rusty paint to remove it. Jane was scraping a run of bubbly paintwork along the housing when Mr Thompson arrived from the deck below. 'More than halfway then,' he said inspecting the stretch of housing and railings that were now bare of paint. 'Jane, put that scraper down for a minute and come over here will you please.' Mr Thompson raised his voice to attract attention. 'You're making a really good job of that. Better than Reynaldo.' 'Whose Reynaldo?' Jane asked as she held the railing to steady herself while walking along the deck. 'Your work mate can tell you who Reynaldo is. Can't you Mike?' 'He started working his passage out of Buenos Aires,' I said, 'but after three days the Radio Officer sent a cable for his parents to pay the fare. It was too much for him working all day. He became a fare paying passenger for the remainder of the trip. He was about your age Jane. 'I couldn't just sit about,' said Jane, 'I've worked since leaving school. Mother's brought a case of books and a half- finished tapestry. She says it's not difficult giving up being a housewife.'

We all three grabbed a railing as the bow pitched into a

larger than average wave. This was followed by a hissing from the disturbed water surging by, as the bow burrowed into the oncoming waves. 'Your mother brought a completed tapestry on to the bridge last night. I assisted in stretching it across a frame,' said Mr Thompson. 'More than a quarter of a million stitches. An incredible amount of work. A knight in full armour with plumed helmet, spear and shield. Very intricate work.' 'I usually get asked to assist mother with that. You're welcome having that job,' said Jane smiling. The Mate ran his hand along the bare metal of the housing, which was rust blotched in places, where sea water had found a way in. 'Ready for wire brushing and a coat of boiled linseed oil before we go any further,' said the Mate, just as the Bosun called out, 'There you are then.' His paint splotched trilby bobbing out of the companionway.

'Will they be having a smoko Mr Mate? This young lass puts the lads to shame. I'm not a just saying that you know. You do your father proud and there—you've only been working at a desk before.' Jane smiled and blushed as the Bosun nodded his head approvingly at the newly cleaned housing. 'You think they deserve a smoko Bosun then,' said the Mate. 'Well, I don't want to be getting on the wrong side of your dad, now do I then,' he said his blue eyes twinkled from beneath his trilby as he turned towards Jane. 'He may decide to cut my beer ration. That would be a disaster now wouldn't it?'

I couldn't argue with that. Nor could Mr Thompson. We both knew how partial the Bosun was to a few cans of beer. 'He expects me to work the same as everyone,' said Jane. 'I wouldn't worry about that.' 'Get your break,' said the Mate. 'Perhaps Bosun you can hand out linseed oil and brushes after their break.' 'I'll be in the paint locker with it ready,' said the Bosun. We placed hammers and scrappers in the paint tins tied to the accommodation hand rail to prevent loss overboard before leaving for our ten minute break. 'Can I be having a word with you Chief about the new wires for the derricks? asked the Bosun. 'Yes Bosun. Clear up your work here before leaving for lunch you two I want you to assist Chippy re-caulking the boat deck this after- noon. He's been re-pitching the planking and needs assistance scraping away residue.' 'Right sir, I said as I followed Jane into the accommodation. 'A change from chipping and scraping paint. He'll show you how it's done,' Mr Thomson called out.

# Chapter 23

# Smoko in the Mess Room

We went to the Engineers Mess Room for our 'smoko.' It was larger than our cabin with an electric boiler plus a sink with washstand and cupboards. At the end a rectangular table, with a fitted bench seat against the bulkhead (wall) by the porthole with additional chairs. On entering, Bill Mackay, the Fourth called across 'How's he treating you Jane? You'd be much better with us down the engine room. Get some intelligent conversation for a start. Look at you, it's a crime. Show me your hands.' Jane held out her hands, covered with red rust and grime before placing them under the tap over the sink, her goggles on her forehead, showing the white clean skin around the eyes. 'I don't mind. I've spent enough time cooped up in offices to last a lifetime. I prefer it out of doors,' she said as she dried her hands on the towel roll 'There you are, I'd have won that bet,' said Leckie (term of address for a ship's electrical engineer) sitting opposite Bill. 'I said you'd prefer being out of doors. I'll be repairing the deck winches later. Perhaps you'd like to assist with something technical for a change?' 'You'll have to ask Mr Thompson first,' said Jane, spooning coffee into a mug. 'Don't like to think you're wasting your life chipping and painting, when you could be doing something more constructive out of doors.' 'It is constructive and I'm not doing it forever. Better than handling bits of paper all day.'

—'Or twiddling with bits of wire, plugs and sockets, eh Jane,' said Bill seeking to get one over on Leckie. 'I didn't say that, I'm quite happy—I've got over being seasick and we're away from winter, and I'm not in a stuffy bank office.'—I felt like saying, 'so there.'

As Jane turned away to fill the coffee mug from the water boiler Leckie stuck his tongue out at Bill. After we made coffee and sat at the mess table, the Second Mate Charlie Brocks came in on the conversation 'Christina's got the better deal,' said Charlie, who sat facing us. 'No thank you. I wouldn't want to be looking at cuts and bruises or getting special meals prepared for a passenger.' 'Nice try Charlie,' said Bill,' but if you'd been married for a year like me, you'd not ever presume to know a woman's opinion about anything. You know Jane I'm just jealous that you work for the other side.' 'How do you mean the other side?' 'I'm not attracted to other women, if that's what you mean.' 'Cooked your goose there,' said Charlie. 'No, no I didn't mean that. You know I didn't love,' said Bill trying to placate Jane. I meant work for the deck side, not the engineering.' 'Why didn't you say that then?' said Jane, plainly enjoying putting Bill on the spot. Charlie stood up. 'That's right Jane, just because you're in the Engineers Mess don't feel you have to pretend to like the idea of being an engineer, or even like them,' he said pulling a face behind Bill, as he went past.

'How are you getting on with that perspective drawing of hatches for ship construction work Mike?' 'It's coming along Sec,' I said, blowing across my coffee mug to cool it down. 'It's easier than drawing the cross section of a water tube boiler.' 'You don't have to do things like that do you?' said Bill, exaggerating a surprised look. 'There was I thinking you just needed to tie a few knots like a boy scout, and know where north and south is on a map.' This was a fairly regular occurrence, Bill having a go at the deck side. Jane seemed to find it amusing. 'We use charts not maps. There's more to it than meets the eye. Careful what you say, Jane might report your comments about future deck officers to her dad,' continued Charlie, grinning across from the sink while washing out his mug. 'Don't be silly. He'd say everyone's entitled to their opinion and provided they did their work professionally they had a right to it. He wouldn't listen to what I said, anyway.'

'Jane you're a chip off the old block. I find your dad a very fair man to deal with,' said Bill. 'Creep,' Charlie replied, calling out, 'see you guys.' He stood aside to let the Third Engineer in. He was tall and athletic looking. 'You'll be able to play football for the ship, won't you Geoff?' said Bill.

'I haven't played in years, but I'll give it a try. It's not premier league stuff is it?' 'Hardly, but we could do with some fresh blood.'

I didn't have the new Third Geoff Hanbury down for being a footballer, but he obviously wanted to fit in. 'Leckie do you still want a hand out on deck,' asked Geoff. 'Geoff you're a hero. I need some help removing winch housings, and replacing some motor parts.' Leckie got up and walked across to join the Third. 'I could do with a bit of sun in my face. It's no problem.' 'Don't want to be nosey Geoff,' said Bill, which of course he was, 'but you don't strike me as a regular Third.' 'No I've been back office for some years. Bit like Jane the office work was getting a bit claustrophobic.' 'I've got a supporter, at last,' said Jane, who turned and smiled at Geoff. I don't think I counted much in the scheme of things, but I was definitely a supporter of Jane's.

I glanced at the clock over the sink, as Leckie and the Third Engineer left together. 'We'd better make a move Jane,' I said, walking across to wash out my mug. We went outside. Down the two companionways to the after deck to collect paint cans of linseed oil, plus brushes from the paint locker at the stern of Albany Princess. 'Now give those rust spots a good wire brush and apply the oil like you're varnishing your very own yacht,' were the Bosun's parting words. This comment amused Jane, but I'd heard "the very own yacht" instruction several times before. We finished and broke for lunch at 1230 hours.

# Chapter 24

# Meeting up with Christina in the Saloon

Jane and Christina usually sat together in the dining saloon. They were already friends before boarding, having agreed to share a flat. Mrs Anderson, The Captain's wife, might point toward Jane, catching her eye, when she considered laughter was a little too boisterous. Christina perhaps telling Jane about an ailment that a member of the crew pretended to have in an attempt to get off work. That, or some joke told to her by a crew member. The deck officers, tended to be more aloof than the engineering officers. Charlie Brocks, the Second Mate was engaged to a doctor, who came on board as soon as we were alongside in the UK. Not, as Tom delicately put it—to give Charlie a medical. The Third Mate, Bill Clifford's marriage was rocky. His ideal world he said, now shattered by the presence of five women on Albany Princess. Mr Thompson, although in his sixties, was in luv, as Tom put it, and engaged to Juliana. His friendliness toward Mrs Anderson, Natalia, perhaps in part because she shared the same nationality as his fiancé. To know what a daughter will be like in later years it's said you need to look at her mother. Natalia was slightly shorter than Jane's five foot seven. Dark haired, but with a strong facial resemblance. Jane, though was blond and with blue eyes like her father. Natalia, must have been at least forty five, but the crew, were adamant that the Captain's wife, was the most attractive woman on board. Natalia Anderson never made aware of how prestigious an accolade she had won.

As an apprentice you were rarely spared the opinions and views of the deck crew about those above deck, so to speak, including passengers. They gossiped and spoke their minds about those they liked or disliked. Jane wasn't in the saloon when I entered. Christina sat three chairs down on the long table. She was wearing a short sleeved dress, her dark hair now reaching her shoulders.

I remembered back to the Electric Hall. Short hair then gave Christina a sort of pixie look, but the extra length I thought made her more attractive. That's what crossed my mind as I sat down anyway. 'What are you looking at Mike?' she asked, which left me speechless for a moment. 'Your hairs grown.' I said. 'How observant of you. Hair grows when it's not cut.' 'I mean it looks good—longer,' I said, unsure whether that was the right thing to say.

The passengers, Eva and Pepe came through the door jabbering in Spanish, but then reverting to English once in the saloon. Eva upset with Pepe. 'We can play and dance all the numbers before the ship reaches B.A. (Buenos Aires). I do not know why you so worry about practice. Can we not rest—from practice, practice, practice?' They sat on the Captain's table.

Apart from the Chief Engineer on the other table we were the only ones in the saloon. The arguing stopped when Wann reached out and held the menu in front of Eva. 'Good day senorita. I hope senorita, will be enjoying rest and would like to place order.' Wann unperturbed by the disagreement between the two of them. I held Wann in high regard for his ability to put his foot in it, but still retain dignity and politeness Christina smiled before saying, 'It's quiet without Tom at lunch.' 'How's Jane getting on Mike, is she all right?' 'I'm the one more used to manual work.' 'No probs,' I said. 'She makes me feel like a slacker. Both the Bosun and Mate are impressed.' 'That doesn't surprise me. Enthusiasm can be wearing though.' I didn't respond. I didn't want to criticise Jane in any way. 'She's happy enough then?' 'Yes, I think so. Why shouldn't she be?' Wann held the menu in front of me. 'I'll have the grilled herring please Wann.' 'Miss Jane, she okay?' he asked lowering the menu holding the chair to steady himself from the ship's movement. 'As far as I know Wann. I expect she'll be here in a minute or two,' said Christina. Wann would join in after hearing only part of a conversation. 'You ask if she's happy Miss Christina?' 'I wish someone was half as concerned about my welfare as you are of Jane Taylor's,' said Christina. 'Miss Devlin would like tea on deck and not in her cabin, this afternoon Wann by the way.' 'Just as you say, Wann can do that. Miss Devlin very amusing lady. I like her as well as Miss Jane.' 'You don't have to make excuses Wann. Can I have some more water please?' 'Of course I fetch now,' he said, picking up the jug with a flourish and making for the saloon galley. 'Why do you ask about her being happy or not?' 'Oh, she broke off an engagement. It's partly why she was so keen to get away from her old life. 'She told me she was bored and stifled working at the bank,' I said. 'I didn't know she was engaged to be married.' The Third Mate and Radio officer entered sitting near to the door. I found it easy talking to Christina, who was down to earth. She turned towards me and placed a hand on the chair seat between us about to explain, but then stopped while Wann placed the grilled herring in front of me. He then went to take orders from the new arrivals.

Christina lowered her voice to a whisper. 'Jane's engagement fell through after she caught her fiancé, an estate agent kissing Veronica the bosses daughter. We were playing badminton and she just happened to go up the stairs to the squash court viewing area and there they were making out. She was engaged and just about to be married and he did that to her?' 'No Mike, not exactly—being engaged doesn't mean getting married immediately, but I got more angry with her boyfriend Terry than she did. It knocked her back. Engagements are expected to lead to marriage, but they can last for years. Unless one party breaks it.—Terry did that all right.' 'Okay,' I said levering the bone from the herring and placing it on the side of the plate. 'Why are you telling me this?' 'Because, because,' said Christina stabbing her fork into a sauté potato before smiling back at me, 'because your eyes light up whenever Jane's name is mentioned.' 'No they don't. How can they?' I said, not wishing to openly show my feelings for Jane.

'Miss Jane, Miss Jane.' Wann caught sight of Jane at the saloon door. 'Wann so glad to see you in his saloon again. You are well?' Jane was almost forced to run rather than walk as the ship rolled. 'You have caught the sun Miss Jane. It's even more beauty making,' said Wann, drawing her chair out from against the table. 'Yes, I'm well, thank you Wann.' 'And happy?' 'Why not Wann?' she said, giving a bemused look before sitting down. 'Nothing. But,'—Christina put her finger on her lips for Wann to shut up. 'Wann is then happy for Miss Jane. One minute fetch menu.' 'Gawd,' said Christina, looking away and letting out a breath before proclaiming—'All hail and welcome to the Princess.'

# Chapter 25

# Jane Keeps the Work Pressure Up

'See you on the Boat Deck then Jane,' I said, pushing back my chair, preparing to leave the saloon. 'That sounds like a private assignation,' said Christina, 'That no one's supposed to know about.' 'It isn't Chris, and you know it—I'm working with Mike—You know that,' said Jane looking piqued. 'Don't take any notice Mike. Yep, I'll be there,' she said smiling politely to indicate that it was Christina she was annoyed with. In my teenage innocence I did believe , she must realize how I felt about her. Christina liked to make out something was going on just to tease. I was aware of that. 'Okay,' I answered before I left. 'We're helping Chippie with re-caulking the Boat Deck.' Christina pulled a face as if in disappointment, before I left for my cabin.

After getting back into working gear I began a rough sketch of the ship at Cape Verde, showing the fuelling tanker alongside with local row boats nearby. Rope lines running to the ship carrying baskets to exchange cartons of cigarettes for carved souvenirs. A simple sketch. The ship recognizable with a blue circle in the red of the funnel. Both done in biro. The pictures of the other boats less effectively drawn. This my second stop at the Islands. I intended keeping a journal of events like port visits aboard Albany Princess. Previously I didn't expect anything particularly eventful to happen, and various projects were in place. Outward bound on my first trip I'd stitched up three grips out of duck canvas. I used the remains of an old grip to measure out the canvas, making it two inches larger to allow for stitching. I chased up library books that crew members had forgotten they'd borrowed. Now with Jane, her mother and father and Christina on board there was much more going on not least my more than crush on Jane, which I wanted to hide from this self – contained world of shipboard life.

The forty minute meal break was up. I put my book, pencils and biros in the drawer. Locked it and withdrew the key. They stayed in there while Jane remained on board Albany Princess. The companionway outside led to the Boat or Funnel Deck so called, for obvious reasons. There was space on both sides of the funnel to play deck golf under corrugated fibre glass canopies. Further forward space for the passengers to sit, read and sunbathe.

When I reached the Boat Deck Angelo and Jane were kneeling over a saucepan precariously positioned on a gimballed gas burner. One side of the saucepan compressed to form a pouring spout. A strong stench like that of melting tar hit me as I walked across. Angelo was smashing a block of pitch into smaller pieces with a small hammer. He turned towards me. 'I make ready for these planks that are now caulked.' They both stood up. The hump on Angelo's back less pronounced when he was standing. 'Will we be helping with this?' asked Jane. 'I show how it is done, but I want you to work on the other side, where it is ready for cleaning up.' The pitch in the saucepan bubbled. Angelo gripped the handle with a gloved hand before trickling melted pitch into the crevice between the planks. The steady uninterrupted sweeping motion of his arm made it look easy. Jane said she fancied having a go, but that was not what we were there for. Angelo moved steadily forwards until the saucepan was empty. 'It is slow process, but we don't have best equipment,' he said placing the saucepan on a metal tray by the gas heater. 'Come with me to other side.' We followed him around to the starboard side, which was sunny. Here the replicated run of decking had rivulets of glistening pitch ready to be scraped flush with the planking We were shown how to angle the scrapers to remove the surplus pitch. Angelo stayed with us to ensure we were sufficiently proficient before returning to the other side. Deck chairs were set up outside the funnel.

I remembered Christina telling Wann that Miss Devlin was having tea on deck. The ship was no longer rolling. The deck steady with a breeze sneaking across from the port side. The railings and stanchions by the lifeboat coated with a fine sand brought in on the wind from the Sahara. The light green wind break of the Bridge was visible above. After about ten minutes Tom stepped out on to the bridge with Eva and Pepe. Charlie Brocks, the Second Mate probably pleased that Tom could speak fluent Spanish. Pepe in a short sleeve navy blue shirt and white trousers. Eva wearing a yellow towelling robe. Pepe pointed to something on deck visible from the bridge, while Eva went into the wheelhouse and reappeared with a cigarette in a pink holder.

Sun glasses glinting in the sun as she stepped down the companionway, unconcerned by the robe opening to reveal a red swim suit and tanned legs. I looked away before Jane noticed me staring. Once on The Boat Deck Eva removed the robe, laying it out on the deck, before knelling and sitting with both hands on raised knees. Head turned to look across at Jane. She placed the cigarette holder on the deck. Jane unaware that she was the focus of attention. A smile flickered on Eva's face, while looking at Jane, but she gave me a threatening look, but turned away on hearing Christina with Miss Devlin.

Christina walked ahead down the companionway. Miss Devlin holding the railing and one of Christina's hands. I didn't like the way Eva was absorbed in looking at Jane. 'Hey Mike, if this was piece work you'd have a wage cut,' she said, unaware of Eva's interest in her. Jane stopped having a go at me when she spotted Christina with Miss Devlin. 'Oh there's Chris and Miss Devlin. I just wouldn't have the patience. I've told mother I'll visit her in a nursing home, but she shouldn't expect me to be any good as a nurse.' It was so totally different from last trip.

I never expected to be working alongside a young woman, like Jane, who I met at a disco dance. I never in my wildest dreams could have imagined a situation like this. Two days later Tom was switched temporarily back on to day work and Jane to work with first Angelo and then the electrician. It was back then to the old routine with Tom picking me up on the way I worked. On reflection though Tom was not as keen to speed on with work as Jane. Bill Mackay was probably right in saying that Jane was a chip off the old block. Once on the Boat deck I heard Miss Devlin say to Christina, 'It's so much nicer out here. The air conditioning is all right, but I feel I might turn into a house plant, dear, stuck indoors. Good there's a hood on that deck chair. A deck chair without a sun hood is like a tennis court without a net. Not really complete.'

Miss Devlin could have been on her way to an outdoor bowls match dressed in a pleated skirt with matching cream cardigan and a red and black scarf with a clasp at the front. Apart from eating in the dining saloon and seeing the passengers relaxing on deck we apprentices were not unlike the servants in a big house invisible unless spoken to. 'Good afternoon Eva. May I join you?' Miss Devlin asked. 'Of course Susan,' she said. 'And Christina. You are so lucky to have Christina. I have escaped from Pepe. He has, how you say?—no conversation, unless it is the work. It is business relationship, no more.' I was getting the hard stare from Jane and returned to the job in hand.

Angelo arrived to check on how we were getting on, before letting us go for a smoko. When we returned a table was placed next to the deck chairs with afternoon tea on a silver tray. Wann asked Miss Devlin if she would be playing deck golf later. I sort of understood what Jane meant when she said she preferred working. There was a limit on how much reading and deck golf you could cope with in three weeks as a passenger on a cargo liner before life became restricted and repetitive. Meal times perhaps becoming the high spot of the day for a passenger.

# Chapter 26

# Entertainment Ahead

Motor Vessel Albany Princess was my first ship, whereas Tom as senior apprentice was familiar with other types of ship. 'It's better on tankers,' he said. 'How's that?' I replied, entering through the bridge door with a bucket and scrubbing brush. 'There're films. The ship gets a box of films- two good ones and usually a third sub- titled rubbishy one. When you hit port they get switched for a new box. 'No library then?' 'What do you want a library for when you've got films?' said Tom. 'Depends whether you like reading or not.' But that argument was lost on Tom. This ship's library held a hundred books. After reading the odd western or science fiction, you ended up reading the others. This was good, in the sense that you read books out of your preferred selection, broadening horizons, to a degree. 'One Norwegian built tanker even had a swimming pool and double bunks.' Tom said, making this seem the height of luxury. The Wheelhouse floor needed clearing and swept ready for hand scrubbing. I carried the rolled up strip of coconut matting outside on to the bridge. Tom swept the dust across with a broom, leaving me to dust pan and brush up the pile in corner of the wheelhouse before we both hand scrubbed the deck with hot water and Atlas. 'You miss the tankers, then,' said the Mate. Mr Thomson, picking up on Tom's conversation from the chart room. 'I didn't actually say that, sir,' said Tom.

Mr Thomson came out to the wheelhouse. 'There's potential boredom, though being on tankers and never getting a proper run ashore,' he said continuing the conversation. 'Definitely agree with that,' said Tom. I was just saying, that cargo liners are a bit sparse for on board entertainment, sir.'

'You're a contradiction Tom Blake.' The Mate would address us by our full name when making a point. He picked up the binoculars before continuing. 'You said, earlier you didn't like the bull on passenger ships, but are envious of the entertainment. It comes with the territory I'm afraid. Passenger ships will always have more entertainment, with higher standards of dress.' Just to prove you wrong though the folk singers have said they will put on an evening concert. First for the sailors and boiler men, next week, but ours will not be until we're nearly off the coast of Argentina.' The Mate scanned the horizon with the binoculars as he spoke. 'Apparently they want a dress rehearsal immediately before arriving at Buenos Aires. There'll be a performance for officers in the Smoke Room. Altogether I think you lads got a pretty good deal this trip. Your dancing partners joining as crew and now—a singing concert. Couldn't get any better I'd say.'

The Mate replaced the binoculars in their case, beneath the wheel house window and returned to the chart room. There were no ships presenting a hazard in sight. Tom kept his voice down from now on. 'There' the judo club I suppose.' I did not pursue that comment. Neither of us excelled at an introductory training session on the mats set up by the funnel. 'I never really understood why Eva and Pepe were over in Britain,' I said. 'They're not that well known.' 'In South America they are. They were probably trying to break into the British and European market. Maybe it didn't work out,' said Tom. 'Anyway I prefer Mantovani's orchestra to folk singing, but one thing—I'll be able to understand the words they sing.' 'True,' I said. Popular modern music like Buddy Holly or the recent new Liverpool band called the Beatles didn't figure on Tom's musical landscape.

I suggested going to see them at the Cavern Club, after meeting an apprentice from another ship, who'd been to see them, but Tom wasn't interested. 'Eva is more than friendly with Jane,' said Tom. 'Christina can't stand her. The way she talks down to her—now. 'What do you mean—talks down to her—now?' 'Apparently, she wanted Christina to apply sun tan lotion. She just handed her the bottle. Turned around, removed her swim suit top and said, 'you can start on my neck and around the bits covered by the top. Then the front. This was in the First Aid Room.' 'Did Christina tell you this?' I asked. 'No, Jane.' 'What happened then?' 'Jane said that Christina was told by the Chief Steward not to apply lotion for burns. That it's classified as self-inflicted when the crew become badly burnt. They're to get another crew member to apply it. Christina suggested that perhaps she could ask Pepe to apply the lotion. Eva's dark skinned and Jane said, Christina told her she wasn't badly burnt, anyway.' 'Tricky. What happened?' I asked. Not an offer a man would have turned down. Opportunity to apply lotion to Eva's skin, even though she was probably nearer thirty than twenty, but this was one woman to another. 'Christina told her what the Chief said.' 'Then what?' 'She stormed out screaming, no young nurse would dare to refuse me like that in Buenos Aires, and spat on the deck outside.'

Just then the Mate called out from the chart room. 'I can't hear any scrubbing, yet.' Tom rattled the bucket of hot soapy water, before picking it up and splashing it around the wheel-house. I grabbed a brush and noisily attacked the froth on the planking, to inform the Mate of work in progress.

# Chapter 27

# Folk Singers Entertain

There was a rolling motion mixed with the pitching of the bow. The plates and cutlery rattled. The Sixth engineer got up out of his chair slowly then speeded his walk to the door. He liked the job, but went ashore after one trip, due to sea sickness. The cork screw motion of the ship did it for him this time. 'You'd think he'd be used to it by now,' said Tom, the hardened sea salt. 'It disturbs the inner ear,' said Christina. 'The sense of balance. It can happen to anyone. You're just lucky Tom.' I was fast becoming anyone. None of us three stayed for the chocolate peach dessert. 'Can't understand it no one wanted the chocolate dessert. I was left on my own. Wann brought a double helping,' said Tom returning from the saloon. 'Big deal,' I said, sprawled on the day bed, considering whether a dash for the toilet in the shower room might be necessary. An irregular crashing noise came from the deck outside.

The door along the corridor opened and slammed shut. A sun burnt hand—fingers spotted with white paint grabbed the cabin door frame. The accompanying face of the Bosun, appeared. 'Then there you are 'tis a fine night for a concert party, to be sure. The Chief has volunteered the both of yous for stage hand work, as I'm told'. 'Yes Bosun,' said Tom in an unenthusiastic voice. 'He's already told me about putting out the deck seats in the Smoke room.' 'They'll be outside. I'll be a leaving then,' said the Bosun.

The rolling and pitching motion ended, as if timed to disturb the evening meal, have a quiet chuckle and go away. Tom stood outside handing chairs over the raised metal entrance. I stacked them outside the smoke room against the bulkhead. 'What time is half time?' asked Wann. He leant out from behind the bar. 'It's not a football match,' said Tom. 'They're due to start in twenty minutes. That's seven and finish before eight. The break will be about seven thirty.' 'Thank you Mr Tom, I prepare squash in jugs, put ice in later. Wann can be front of game.' 'Don't you mean ahead of the game?' I suggested to Wann. 'That's right Wann is at the head of the game.' 'Leave it,' said Tom. 'Don't encourage him, he'll want to take part in the singing next.'

Earlier Chippy had hammered together planks over a base to form a triangular stage and covered it with ply. It fitted into the corner of the smoke room. The pelmet at the front looked suspiciously like rag waste painted blue and white, cut into flag shapes. Cargo cluster lights improvised as spots strung above by the electrician. Improvised screens made from Duck canvas tacked on to battens made for a dressing room area. A poster of a Gaucho in the Pampas swinging a bolas to catch a black and white steer, spread across one screen. Another of Eva and Pepe performing on a stage in Buenos Aires.

'You can't sit in the three front rows, and there's no smoking.' Tom told the Fourth and Second engineer as they came in. 'There's a surprise said Bill we don't get a choice of seats.' 'And there's no smoking in the "smoke" room,' chipped in the Second.—'No, no, I understand they'll both be singing. It makes sense. I'll probably not be able to stay to the end. I can sneak out from the back,' he said to Bill. The Chief Steward came in with programmes printed on the back of menu cards to hand out. Pepe and Eva followed him—both with two guitar cases. Eva now dressed in black slacks, but with sparkling dresses across the guitar cases. They disappeared behind the screens to prepare. 'Can't see the point of handing out programmes,' said Tom. 'They'll be asking me to translate the song titles into English.' 'The only one they'll recognize will be Guantanamera. I don't know the translation, anyway. Here Mike put a card on each chair and be done with it.' Tom handed me the cards, which I placed on the chairs as the Radio Officer, the Chief Engineer and the Devlin's arrived. Miss Devlin was assisted by her brother Dennis and the Second Steward to her seat. The clock above the bar with gold strips emulating the sun said seven twenty. Captain Anderson, Mrs Anderson, Jane, and Christina arrived at seven twenty five. Mrs Anderson chatted to Tom in Spanish. 'You two can sit at the back by the light switches,' said Captain Anderson to us. 'The door will need closing—there's light from on deck coming from that set of curtains. 'He pointed to the side of the stage. I went to close them—the cold from the blower above chilling my face as I reached to flick them across. The Chief Steward entered and walked past me just as the strumming of a guitar came from behind the screens. Perhaps a prearranged signal to inform the Chief, as promoter, that the performers were ready.

'Ladies and Gentlemen we are privileged this evening to have performing live for us two of Argentina's most popular folk singers and dancers, here on board Albany Princess. Please give a warm welcome to Eva and Pepe.' There was applause from the audience of about fifteen, as the Chief Steward sat in the row next to Mrs Anderson. It was the Third Mate who called for lights prompted by the Chief steward—'Lights.'

A guitar picked out the melody from behind the screen of Guantanamero, a song which was popular in Buenos Aires. The playing stopped, then started again with a vigorous strumming. Pepe appeared dressed Gaucho style with white sombrero and red neck tie, He walked forward with measured steps matching the strident insinuating strum from his guitar. Eva followed in a red Flemenco dress, silver sparkling from the white dress trim. Black hat, set back on her head. Hair sculpted in a ponytail. The heavy mascara, and pencilled brows, accentuating black eyes. She stood next to Pepe, dress twirling, head held high as she struck the floor with her feet.

Red finger nails flashed in the light and castanets clicked to the strum of Pepe's guitar. The tempo slowed.

'For you now a Paraguayan love song,' called Pepe, which they sang, without any dance steps.

# Chapter 28

# Half Time and Afterwards

'We now to have ten minute break. Request smokers to go to deck. You will understand smoke is not good for voice,' said Pepe clutching his throat and coughing to demonstrate the fact. 'Diez minutos, por favor.' 'Ten minutes only,' called out the Chief Steward, as I switched on the main lights. The wood slated bar cover rattled up.

Alcohol was consumed in cabin quarters at sea. Soft drinks only available at the bar this evening. Crew members were rationed to three cans of beer or lager a day. Officers a case of beer or a half bottle of spirits. The lower deck separated like second class passengers on a train, but if anything with fewer privileges. The bar was stocked with alcohol in port for entertaining dignitaries. Bill, the Fourth Engineer in marrying a local girl from Cordoba was allowed to invite the parents of the bride and close friends to the smoke room for a party. Alcohol available at the bar while the ship was alongside in Buenos Aires. The guests taking empty lager and beer cans home as momentos. Lager and beer was only produced in bottles in Argentina at the time.

The Second Steward stood behind the bar in white jacket and gold epaulettes. Wann brought tall glasses half- filled with orange and lemon squash, to the bar counter. 'It is orange or lemon squash—now with ice,' said Wann, making it sound like a treat. There was a slight pitching as the ship progressed at fourteen knots. The polished wood panelling across the outer bulkhead in the Smoke Room creaked as the ship's bow rose and fell into the head sea. The glasses on the trays clinked intermittently with the pulse from the main engine.

Tom and myself were first outside with orange squash. Tom,

cigarette in hand, passed his glass to me. He cupped his hand around the Lucky Strike lighter as the flame spurted out, giving me a share of the stench of both lighter fuel and tobacco, as he breathed out smoke from nose and mouth. I looked down at the sprinkled phosphorescence, as it danced in the bow wave. 'They're good Mike. I can see why they're popular in Buenos Aires. Flamenco blends in with the folk songs. They've got a mix of old and new. Popular music with a Spanish fieriness. 'I didn't realize you were such an expert,' I said 'They seem like the genuine article,' said Tom, taking sips of orange juice with cigarette and glass in hand. 'So you've changed your mind , then,' I said 'what do you mean?' 'Well when we met Jane and Christina by the taxi, you said, you were unsure about them. You said they just didn't seem right.' 'I don't remember that.' 'Well you did,' I said, 'Anyhow we'd better get back inside, we're responsible for switching the main lights off. 'Long as one of us is there. Catch you up,' said Tom.

I walked towards the door. It opened before I reached for the handle and the Third Engineer, Geoff Hanbury came out on deck. 'Enjoying the show?' he asked. 'Just came up for a breather,' he continued, lighting the cigarette already in his mouth. 'Yes,' I said. He lent on the railings opposite a port-hole. The one I drew the curtain on, which was now slightly ajar. 'You're missing out being on watch.' 'Not a great music fan Mike,' he said. 'I'm looking forward to the football when we reach Buenos Aires,' he said, as I stepped inside. Just as Pepe waved his hand to indicate for the lights to be switched off, Tom nipped into a seat by the door. 'We are back again in Argentina. I will strum my guitar to attract a dancer perhaps,' announced, Pepe. After about thirty seconds of intricate guitar playing, Eva appeared from behind the screen wearing a red topped dress with a black split skirt. Black hair now curled seductively over her left shoulder. Much of her right leg provocatively displayed during the rhythmic dance steps. The

Sixth Engineer gave a subdued whistle, which suggested his sea sickness was no longer in control. The clicking castanets synchronized with the steps gave powerful stage presence. Eva was dancing in front of the screen, when the guitar strumming abruptly ceased. 'We lack a tambourine player for our next song, don't we Eva?' said Pepe.—'Me gustaria que lo hicieras.' 'He wants someone from the audience,' Tom translated for me sat next to him at the back. 'Preferably a woman to just shake the tambourine—when I indicate by tapping the case of my guitar. It is easy. But to contrast with the dark Latin look, a fair haired woman with perhaps blue eyes.' That narrowed the field significantly. 'Ah, I see there is a person. Would you Jane help us with our next song? The tambourine will complete the enjoyment of it.' Jane was already sitting near to the front. She stood up. 'Applause for our new musician, if you please ladies and gentlemen,' Pepe called out. We clapped, but others in the audience gave a cheer and there was an isolated whistle, from Andrew, the Fifth engineer. Eva went behind a screen and returned with a tambourine above her head tapping it with her other hand. Pepe held out his hand to assist Jane from floor to stage. 'Muchas gracies senorita,' he said smiling and bowing... 'I need to change guitar I will fetch it. Uno momento.' He went out of view behind the screen, leaving Jane with Eva.

'It's easy, mon cherie, every time Pepe taps you follow with the tambourine. Like this,' said Eva shaking the tambourine and hitting it with her other hand. 'Yes, I know how to do it. I did that in school,' said Jane. I didn't like the 'mon cherie' It seemed too familiar. How a man or woman might address a young lover. Jane's tone of voice indicated I felt that she didn't like it either. 'It is better and better,' replied Eva, undisturbed by the remark. It didn't seem at that time anyway unusual that Pepe would leave the stage to change guitars. This particular act was unrehearsed and for all we knew spontaneous.

I have to admit my eyes were only on Jane. Hair made even more fair by the sun. The short skirt and sleeveless top allowing light to catch her skin. Not fiercely burnt, but a coffee shade. I sensed the quiet in the room when she first stepped on to the stage. Sailors dream about mermaids, visiting their ship. For me Jane surpassed any such vision. We were no longer strangers, but friends following on from that first meeting at the Electric Hall, I considered. I wished to be more than a friend, even though I'd been told I was like a young brother. I wasn't aware of Pepe's return immediately. A shocked gasp of horror came from the audience before I noticed him. When I did the friendly musician style had gone. In each hand he held black rifles. Their black webbed straps hung beneath. No one saw this coming. Both of them superb actors. The singing and dancing a foil for their true identities. Eva grabbed Jane by the arm, a look of triumph on her face, dropping the tambourine as Pepe passed a rifle over. He knelt and raised the rifle to firing position. Bill Mackay stood up seemingly unafraid of the rifle pointing in his direction. 'Leave her alone,' he said. Natalia, her mother called 'Jane,' in a painful, shocked voice and got to her feet. 'Sit down. No one to move or we kill the girl. Be quiet. You do exactly what I say or she dies. His voice was if anything quieter than previously.

Pepe moved the barrel to point at Jane and back at the audience as he spoke. 'Do I make myself clear?' 'Leave my daughter alone, she's done nothing, she's an innocent girl,' Natalia called out visibly shocked and stunned by what was happening as was everyone in the room, save for the terrorists. Captain Anderson remained silent. 'Ha, we have your attention, now I see,' said Pepe with a cruel smile. It was a reverse chrysalis situation. The singing and dancing butterflies changed into malevolent beings. Pepe's gun threat and subdued yet menacing voice stunned the room into silence. Tom whispered, 'they're AK 47s'. I can tell by the curved magazine holder and pistol grip, as if identifying some special make of car.

I remembered the look of bewilderment on Jane's face, when her arm was grabbed and how she tried to pull away, but stopped when Pepe strode out from behind. The nightmarish events that followed still fresh in my mind. 'You, apprentice cadet switch on the light now.' Pepe waved the barrel up and down in my direction as he made the order. Captain Anderson looked backwards and said, 'Do as he says, lad.' He had his arm around Natalia, who was bent forward. Apart from a repeated sobbing sound there was quiet in the room. Jane looked more concerned for her mother than herself. I was quick to switch on the lights. Pepe rose from a knelt shooting position to his feet and stood to attention. The gun barrel only momentarily vertical, before panning forward towards those of us sat in the audience. Eva let go of Jane's arm prodding her forward with the gun barrel, making her into a part human shield, while still pointing the rifle forwards. She appeared prepared to use the rifle should the need arise. More so than Pepe, I felt. Even so her sparkling dress twinned with a gun might be seen as a scene from a fashion photo shoot in another context.

Pepe went once more to a presenting arms position, but then with the gun held out in front, announced. 'We are Freedom Fighters For Las Malvinos. I take custody of your ship Captain Anderson. Your daughter is our hostage, who will stay with us—and you Radio officer,' he said waving the gun at Mr Jones—'bring two chairs on to the stage. You also are hostage. It is not known by your company Captain, but part of the cargo in Number Three hold is guns and ammunition. I need to move the ship to a position near to Mar del Plato. From now I am El Capitana. I believe you will cooperate Paul. Love conquers all. Is that not an English expression? The ship is just an object—not alive. No one need be killed or injured,' he said, as if he was leading a party of walkers along a mountain path. There was resignation in Captain Anderson's voice when he next spoke.

In calling him by his first name, you felt Pepe had already in some way undermined the Captain's authority. 'I will cooperate fully, but you're assuming we are alone in these waters. For how long do you expect to get away with this? There is a British naval presence in the area.' 'Why Paul we have the Radio Officer and I need for you to run the ship as normal. To signal when you need to your company. To not give any indication that anything is other than normal.' The Radio Officer and Jane were sat in chairs with Eva standing behind Jane 'You will not want anything to happen to either of these crew members. Your beautiful daughter, especially.' Jane I could see was both shocked and bewildered by the horrific changes of Pepe and Eva from singers to terrorists.

The Radio Officer's fear revealed in his rigidity as he sat next to Jane. I felt more anger than fear. 'We are expecting full cooperation from you Radio Officer,' said Pepe. Sparks looked towards Captain Anderson in a manner best described as abject terror. 'We'll do as he says Mr Jones,' said Captain Anderson. The Radio Officer nodded his head, vigorously, but did not speak. 'Bueno, that is muy bueno Paul.' The terrorists moved the gun barrels slowly in an arc, from left to right and back again to take in everyone in the room.

'You understand we are politically neutral. None of my crew are involved in this dispute. Some on board aren't British or Argentinean nationals. We're just going about our lawful business,' Captain Anderson replied, after removing his arm from around Natalia.

# Chapter 29

# Albany Princess under Terrorists' Control

'No problema, Paul, it's like temporary delay. Like for you delay at a railway station. The train not arrived. All different peoples have to wait. It is for you to wait while our special cargo is unloaded. That is all. You will go with us to the bridge Paul, with Senora Anderson, the Radio Officer and Senorita Jane. We go as party.' He shouldered the AK47 and I saw the light catch the knife blade he produced from his jewelled waistcoat. 'Don't move, any of you,' said Eva ensuring we knew she was still covering us. Pepe walked over to Jane and placed the blade against her cheek. She flinched and turned her face sideways. A gasp of horror came from the room. 'I remind you all that we control this ship. I am Capitan. For your daughter's face to stay as beautiful, we expect loyalty to our cause from everyone. I make myself clear do I not?' Captain Anderson stood up, powerless, spreading his hands to show they were empty. We all knew that there was no choice, but to comply. For all Pepe's protestation that he was now the Captain I never thought Captain Anderson capitulated. It was like a game of chess where in this case sensible talking could play a part in avoiding injury or even death.

'I'm prepared to take my ship to your discharge destination as soon as humanly possible. And in return I ask you not to harm Jane or any of my crew. We have no disagreement with your aims. We're just ordinary seaman going about our work.' He sat back down in his chair and Natalia smiled at him, having regained composure from the initial horror and most likely understanding the need to defuse the tension.

I admired the way Captain Anderson was able to make it seem that the incident could be treated as like a course

119

alteration that really didn't interfere with anything going on in the running of his ship. A display of understated courage when I look back on the hijack. 'That's good Paul. That is well said. I need all in ship to agree with you Capitan Anderson. Chief Steward before we leave for the bridge you are to inform others of the situation. We will not hesitate to shoot any person who obstructs our mission. Comprende? Chief Steward.' 'Si senor Pepe,' said the Chief in a somewhat obsequious manner, I thought. Captain Anderson stood up. 'Do as he says Chief Steward send your staff to all cabins and the Seaman's Mess room and say we have to make a detour. Make it known that the ship is being captained by Pepe and is temporarily off route, but they're to perform duties as normal.

'Chief,' he continued turning to Chief Engineer Harper, 'You're best placed to contact the engine room and members of your staff.' 'I'll see to that Captain Anderson, be assured of that,' he replied.

'That is excel-enty, Paul. It is good beginning for me to have someone like you with understanding and sense. Before we leave I give the Chief Steward help for to say what has happened.' The Chief was holding his arm around Mrs Anderson's chair comforting her, while sat next to her on the other side. It was Christina afterwards who said the plan to take over the ship was masterly, in that, apart from the Mate who was on the bridge, all the senior officers were in the room including Captain Anderson. The taking of Jane as the main hostage in front of them focused attention on the true horror of the situation.

The appreciation that there was no alternative but to cooperate in discharging the munitions stored in Number Three Hold made clear from Jane being taken hostage. The ship was in the control of Eva and Pepe, effectively hijacked. The crew needed to be made aware of the situation as early as possible to prevent anyone being foolish enough to resist. I felt that there was never any doubt that these two would open fire immediately, if they felt their demands were not being met. Pepe left the stage holding the Ak47 in the air. He walked past Tom and me and out on to the deck. The burst of gun fire into the night air was deafening. 'There,' he said on returning, 'that is a statement for all the ship, that is not here. They will believe what you say more easily—go Chief Steward, Chief Engineer. Now everyone else is to return to their cabins and continue with duties as normal. We leave. You two go now to tell crew.' He waved his gun at the two Chiefs. Chiefs Davies and Harper.

'I need for a signal to Montevideo—there is engine trouble that the ship is stopped. It is something you do Paul? It must be normal, si? To the port authority, comprende?' 'I can have the Radio Officer send a signal,' said Captain Anderson. 'It is something that does happen.' 'Muy bueno, but to say not needing assistance, eh,' said Pepe. 'To say it is something engineers can fix. I will be with you when this signal is sent. I was—how you say commander in Argentinean navy—you should never try to be clever with me. We need time for ship to go to Mar del Plata. That there is delay, but no one is looking. When we go to bridge we set new course. I have exact position for the ship to go to. We select new course to unload on to my boats outside of Mar Del Plato. Paul you lead the way through the accommodation with Senora Anderson.' Eva, with a pistol in her hand, the AK 47 across her shoulder followed with Jane and the Radio Officer.

Seconds later two shots followed, interspersed with a cry and the clatter of a heavy object. When I looked down the corridor the Electrician was on the floor, blood staining the white of his boiler suit, a stillson nearby. You could say it was foolhardy, but if Eva had been slower responding the wrench would have landed on Pepe's head. It was a spur of the moment decision, but others could have been injured. The

121

Electrician was in the Engineer's Mess, perhaps shaken into action after Pepe's burst of fire. With the Smoke Room door open it was possible to hear what was being said. I remembered later about Leckie mentioning that there was a box of tools in the cupboard under the sink. One of four boxes, he said that were—'Strategically placed where people do stupid things with electrical equipment.' This time it could be said he did a stupid thing in grabbing the wrench to use as an attack weapon.

'What the hell was that?' I heard the Captain shout back from the end of the corridor. Pepe was nearer to us and said, 'It was a stupid attack Paul. It will be as warning to others. Your Electrician wanted to be brave. It is all right no one else is hurt. Jane and your Radio Officer are safe with Eva to guard them.' That seemed a contradiction, where without the hijack everyone would be safe, but for terrorists this creates a psychologically protective bubble around the hostages, by making enemies of all outside their hostage group. There was a stunned silence from us all in the smoke room.

'Let no one else be so foolish'. Pepe said. 'We continue to the bridge. The nurse can see to him—gracie Eva, that you have your shooting skills with you. Your dancing needed much rehearsing.' A back handed compliment, if ever there was one—not though at the time upsetting Eva. 'I am alive again. Not having to sing and dance, pretending to be like plaything for men—It's escape from a prison,' she shouted back.

I could only just make out Pepe's voice as he turned back towards Captain Anderson and said 'It is now important you and crew cooperate. It's poss-ib-le he can see a doctor within twenty four hours. Our cargo will be unloaded tomorrow morning off the coast on to open barges and you will be able to summon help. Let us have no more again incidents, like this, eh Paul. You hear what I say—all of you.' A sneering loudly spoken riposte, articulated for the benefit of those of us left in the smoke room. Jane I could see wanted to help. 'Leckie,' she called out arms reaching towards his crumpled body, but then pulled aside by Eva. 'Your nurse friend, she can see to him. I hit only in shoulder and leg' 'You bitch,' said Leckie on the deck holding his left shoulder. Blood having spurted from the wound on to bulkhead and deck. The blood stain spreading on the leg of his white boiler suit. 'Keep move,' Eva said to Jane and the Radio Officer—making them step over his legs as he held his right hand over his shoulder in an attempt to stop blood loss.

They went up the companionway by which time Christina had dashed with a cloth from the bar, getting Leckie to hold it against his shoulder, before ripping open the first aid box in the Mess Room. Tom and I joined her. A dressing was wrapped around the shoulder wound after Christina cut away the arm of his boiler suit with the first aid scissors. We helped her lean him against the bulkhead. 'Won't be wearing this boiler suit again,' he said as the trouser leg was cut away below the knee to apply a dressing and staunch the flow of blood. 'Get some blankets and pillows,' Christina said. 'Use mine son. Just three doors down,' Leckie said, sounding calm. There were several engineers in the corridor and I heard Charlie, the Second Mate say, 'You'd best return to your cabins or duties. Christina needs air to work in.' I went to fetch blankets and pillows, thinking that he's talking and aware of what's going on. Is this what they mean by flesh wounds was what came to mind—never having assisted in bandaging a person with gunshot wounds before. I returned with blankets and two pillows. After the corridor cleared Leckie, said 'He's not that badly hurt'. I was then thinking. 'There's a lot of blood, but it's his lower leg and left shoulder. He's talking and aware of what's going on.' Leckie said, 'I could do with a cigarette.' Christina had finished bandaging the wounds to stop the blood flow. She wrapped a blanket around and we lifted him from the deck on to a pillow. Charlie said 'Good try Leckie. You'll soon be mended old son.' 'No liquids or cigarettes' said Christina. 'Not yet anyway. Can I leave you with Tom and Mike I need to get more medical supplies. We'll get you to your cabin then to rest. 'I'm okay,' he said. 'I can hold on, but be back soon, love.' 'I will,' she said ushering me and Tom into the Mess Room. Both of us with only basic first aid training. Charlie stayed with him in the corridor. 'Look you need to keep him talking.' I don't know how much blood he's losing. There could be internal bleeding. Charlie can come with me to the Sick Bay to fetch more bandages and pain killers. He really needs immediate hospital care.'

After they left Leckie said, 'light us a ciggie Mike, there's a good lad. 'Tom make us some tea.' 'I'll light a ciggie for you,' said Tom. I looked at Tom with surprise. Tom was quiet, but somehow more understanding of the nature of the situation than I must have been. He lit the cigarette giving it to me to pass to the blanketed figure. Leckie inhaled and blew the smoke out. 'I'll make a mug of tea,' Tom said. There can be a feeling of security in ritual and this was one of those times. Tom went into the Mess Room. Leckie wanted to talk.

'I couldn't stop myself. I heard the little bastard's threats,' he said quietly but clearly. 'I've a lad about your age and a daughter a bit older, should think,' he said confidingly. Out of nowhere, he then said, 'You love that girl don't you?' 'Christina d'you mean?' I replied. 'No, no, not the nurse— Jane, of course. I've seen you with her. I'm out there on deck working. It doesn't take like an expert to see the change in you this trip—and it ain't just the sea air. You might hide it from the world, you think.' He coughed and blood trickled from the corner of his mouth. I felt scared, but tried not to show it. He didn't appear to be aware of the blood and took another puff on the cigarette handing it back. 'I feel really tired now Mike. Tell Christina I tried to stay awake. His head slumped to one side and he slid from the pillows supporting his body half raised against the bulkhead.

The noise of the engine seemed to grow louder, but I was probably unaware of it while listening to Leckie. Cigarette smoke mixed with cooking smells, still in the corridor from the evening meal. 'Tom, Tom I called out. 'What do we do. He's fallen asleep and Christina said try to keep him awake. Tom came out from the mess room. He went to the other side where his face had turned. Tom knelt and called 'Leckie,' before seeing his eyes. Leckie's face appeared pale. I noticed that much. 'He's gone further than just sleep Mike. Come and look at his eyes.' I did as Tom asked. I just said, 'No he can't be.' His eyes open and staring when I looked. 'He was talking to me a minute ago.' I'd never seen a person die, but Tom had somehow spotted the run up. I hadn't. 'Sit in the Mess Room Mike. There's nothing we can do.'

Shortly afterwards the door opened from the outside deck and Tom went to meet Christina and Charlie who were returning with the bandages 'He's gone Chris,' I heard Tom say. 'He can't have,' said Charlie. I came out into the corridor. The blood was congealed and darker on the bulkheads and across the tiles in the corridor. 'Arteries were severed, and there was a lot of blood loss,' said Christina. 'I hoped the bandaging might have stopped further bleeding.' It was Charlie who rushed for the toilets to be sick.

I still found it hard to believe that Leckie was talking one minute and gone the next. 'We heard gunshots, what's happened?' the Chief Steward called from the end of the corridor with the Second Steward following him. 'It's Leckie,' said Tom, 'he's copt it—he's dead.' 'Jeez,' said the Second. 'It's like a blood bath.' 'He had a go at Pepe and Eva shot him,' continued Tom.

'The body will need to be stitched in canvas and go in the meat fridge,' said the Chief. He sounded matter of fact, but it needed someone like the Chief, to straight away assess the situation. His response suggested that managing death on board was not new to him. He didn't allow us to dwell on the situation. 'Mop, cloths and a bucket of hot soapy water are needed Second Steward and Christina you can accompany me to the sick bay to fetch the stretcher. Charlie came out of the toilets.

'Glad you're here Chief,' 'I'll see to this Charlie,' he replied. Leadership devolves rapidly in emergencies to those who can assess and take appropriate action. Chief Steward Davies was such a person. Charlie was due on watch at midnight and I was at four. It was the Chief Steward who said, 'Christina and Tom you stay and help You two best get some rest.' Charlie's reaction to the death and my inexperience not making us best choice to be in his team. We were surplus to requirements.

Charlie was on watch at midnight and needed sleep and I was due back on watch keeping duties, later. My watch was the four to eight tomorrow. We should have been approaching Montevideo. Now, according to Pepe we were to head for Mar del Plato. Tom, again, wangled to stay on day work, with his story about needing study time. This meant he would still get a night's sleep. Although horrified by what had happened to Leckie I was more worried for Jane's safety, but I went to asleep immediately my head touched the pillow.

# Chapter 30

# Awakened Early

A tapping on the porthole woke me. I lay awake first wondering why I was awake. Then the tapping restarted. I pulled back the sheet and lowered myself on to the cabin deck. There was a deck head light outside, which meant a chink of light escaped between the gap in the two curtains across the porthole. I half opened the curtains and in the middle of the porthole was a small white ensign. This was removed and I could see a blackened face with a tight fitting black beret. This person placed a finger to his lips. I was sufficiently awake to understand the message of the White Ensign. It was the Royal Navy. I turned the wing nuts on the porthole and opened it. 'Lieutenant Rob Payne from Resolution, You are? He demanded. His breathless voice a loud whisper. 'Mike Peters, apprentice,' I said rubbing my eyes—'How on earth did?' 'Can't explain now, need to get off this deck. Open that door will you?' He pointed to the outside door. The one I went through on my way to the bridge. 'Only if the coasts clear and no one's in the corridor. No armed terrorists.' 'They went to the bridge before I turned in,' I replied. 'Need to meet with your Third Engineer,' he continued. 'Right, don't go away,' I said, which immediately seemed a stupid thing to say. I closed the porthole and curtains. Grabbed my dressing gown from the wardrobe and not bothering with shoes stepped out into the corridor.

Other than the engine's constant pulsating and the corridor light dancing from the vibrating bulkhead opposite, all was quiet. I checked that there was no one in the mess room, the horror of the shooting the night before coming back to me. The body now taken away and the blood cleaned away from the deck and bulkheads. I noticed a large blood spot still on the cover of an overhead light. The only evidence that remained of what had happened.

Lieutenant Payne was flattened against the bulkhead when I opened the door, but made himself visible. He needed to be sure that I was the one opening the door. 'I'll follow you, but step backwards if you hear or see anyone,' he said. Only then did I notice the Lieutenant was wearing a black wet suit. On the right leg an unclipped black holster, the revolver handle visible. Beneath this was a sheath moulded into the leg of the wet suit, displaying the black handle of a knife. We were inside the cabin within seconds. 'Leave the lights off,' he said, holding a torch adjusted to a low light. He sat on the day bed. I on the chair by the desk. 'They've shot and killed the electrician,' I said. 'Last night after taking hostages. The woman shot him in the corridor.' 'Yes we know about that from the Third Engineer. We're in radio contact.' 'The replacement Third?' I interrupted 'Well yes he's more than an engineer. He's employed by the intelligence services MI6. The Admiralty directed us to close in and gain radio contact. We've been shadowing you,' he said removing the black beret, which revealed wiry ginger hair and a white streak where face blackening met the hairline. 'After the terrorists took over in the Smoke Room he contacted us. We've been in radio contact, since your ship moved into these waters.' 'That makes sense,' I said. 'He was standing outside on the deck having a smoke. He must have heard what happened.' 'Yep. After they produced rifles in the Smoke Room and took hostages, he contacted us and then again after the shooting.' He said this in a matter of fact sort of way, as if he'd just walked up the gangway. 'We waited till we got the signal that there was no one on the starboard side of the bridge, likely to see us or in view of the ship's stern and drew up alongside in a launch.' Lieutenant Payne rolled back the rubber sleeve on the left arm of his wet suit.

The luminescent green arrowed hands on the watch pointed at 3.30. Another day. 'Heck the twelve to four watch will be knocking to get me up in ten minutes.' I said. 'Where's the Third Engineer's cabin, exactly. It is in this corridor, isn't it?' said the lieutenant. 'He's expecting me.' 'The same side, but a little way down,' I replied. 'There's a plaque on the door. What's going to happen?' I asked. 'Act as normal. What are your duties?' 'I'm on lookout from six to eight, but will be on the bridge at four—probably on the wheel.' 'The Third Engineer is he due to go on watch?' 'Yes. He's on the same four to eight, but in the engine room.' 'He may have a boiler suit I can change into to hopefully move about, unnoticed, if necessary. The plan is for him to light a cigarette and lean over the after accommodation railings on the portside when it appears safe. My men can vacate the stern locker room and move forward into the mid-ships accommodation.

'At seven smoke should pour from the engine skylights. A call will be made to the bridge that a fire has broken out in the boiler room and becoming uncontrollable. Got that?' 'Yes,' I replied 'You'll be able to confirm this from your look out position on the Monkey Island, reporting the smoke— that is. Here,' he opened a flap at the top of the wet suit and produced the little white ensign, turning it over. There was a black background, but in bright white lettering the words- Royal Navy Aboard. 'You say you will be wheelman at the beginning of the watch?' he asked. 'Yes,' not understanding where this was going. 'We really need to make your officer of the watch aware that we are on board.'

He handed over the small white ensign. 'You should be able to draw him to the wheel. You got the message when you saw the flag. There's the writing on the other side, as well. Place it on the compass binnacle or somewhere without the terrorists seeing. Do you think you'll be able to do that?' 'Yes,' I said, 'there's only the two of them, but it depends where they are on the bridge.' 'I appreciate that, but you should be able to get the officer of the watch to stand next to the wheel at some point by alerting him to some change. Do your best Mike. When the diversion from the smoke starts at seven we really need the officer of the watch to be aware we're on board and about to regain control.' 'Now you've explained things— that you're going to surprise them. Disarm them—I'll do my best,' I said. 'Good lad Mike, I'm sure you'll be able to cope.' I did not share all of the Lieutenant's confidence. 'One last thing, 'Lieutenant Payne said, before leaving 'At seven, when on lookout report smoke from the engine room skylights to the bridge, regardless of whether there is any or not. Got it?' 'Yes, I said. 'Good Luck.' 'And you ,' I replied.

'Open the door. Check the coast is clear Mike.'

# Chapter 31

# Terrorists on the Bridge

I returned to my bunk although very much awake. I felt that I needed to make out I was asleep when the watch called. About eight hours had passed since Pepe and Eva hijacked the ship, if those were their real names. There were unanswered questions. Not least how were they allowed to continue as passengers, if MI6 knew they were terrorists? Or did they know? I could now see why Pepe and Eva's show was delayed, until we were nearly at Montevideo and near to Mar del Plato on the other side of the River Plate.

I shivered involuntarily. Not that muscle relaxing shake before you fall asleep, but a shiver brought on thinking about Leckie. Not realizing he was dying, while talking about his children and then how he'd spotted my feelings for Jane. I feared for her safety more than anything else. The killing of Leckie perhaps motivated the Royal Navy to board. A frightening realization dawning that Jane's life might have been been less at risk if no boarding had taken place and the armaments in Number Three hold discharged off Mar del Plato. The ship allowed to continue back to Montevideo. They were arguably taking only what belonged to their freedom fighting party, albeit illegally stowed on board. These thoughts flowed through my mind in the minutes between Lieutenant Payne leaving to meet up with the Third Engineer and the knock on the cabin door.

It was Fred. 'You awake? How awake?' I mumbled 'yes' to the first question. 'Awake enough to listen to what I'm telling you?' he continued. I switched on the reading light above my bunk and sat up turning towards Fred while blinking at the light flooding in from the corridor outside. He—now with hands holding the door frame either side and turned towards where I lay in my bunk. 'I've not been that much asleep, Fred. Miss Taylor, Is she all right?' 'I sort of guessed you'd be wanting to know that,' he said. I couldn't see why, he'd guess that. 'It's normal up there, but in a kind of horrible way—if you get my meaning. The wheelhouse doors are rattling something shocking. Pepe's said the engine's to stay on maximum revs to get to the Mar del Plato rendezvous as soon as possible, wherever that is. Charlie's got to stay to get a star position. Pepe's been saying he was a Captain in the Argentine Navy—so he says.' 'Yes Fred, but Jane, I mean Miss Taylor, is she all right?' 'Brave lass gives as good as she gets. They've got her and Sparky in the chart room on the day bed, trussed up like kippers. Well Sparky is. That Eva when she speaks to Miss Taylor she's sort of all sweet with her. Nasty bit of work. Not seen the likes of 'er before. Don't want to again. The other one struts about, but she's pure evil. The way she shot Leckie. Chills you through and through it does.'

'Okay Fred, so is there a wheelman?' 'Oh, yes you'll be wanted on the wheel. Are you awake now? Said I'd help the Chief with the body. He's wanting a canvas cover sewn up down the side. The boys are saying they're wanting overtime money. Compensation for armed conflict. I told them if they play up I'll be the one doing overtime, sewing them into body bags.'

'Good advice Fred,' I said, 'I'll be up there by four. No need to call me again.' I was a bit stunned. It was the longest conversation I'd ever had with Fred. The good news was that Jane was uninjured and coping. It was five to four when I left my cabin for the Bridge. The deck wet from rain. About eight and a half hours had elapsed, since the hijack in the smoke room. The blast of air from the engine room extract fan as I walked across the Boat deck reminded me of my meeting with

Lieutenant Payne and his plans to create a smoke diversion later that morning. How I needed to alert Mr Thompson that the Navy were on board without giving the game away to the terrorists. It was dark in the wheelhouse.

My shoes squelched on the damp deck. I made out the figures of Charlie and Mr Thompson standing in front of the wheelman. Pepe in the far corner sitting on a high stool, which the officer of the watch might sit on when the Captain was not on the bridge. The AK 47 hooked by its strap on a window lever in easy reach from where he sat. Boxes of ammunition on the deck nearby. Mr Thompson held up his hand for me to wait. Pepe looked across—'stay there,' he shouted. 'Hey Eva,' he called out. 'Are you awake?' 'Of course. What is it?' Her voice coming from the chart room behind. 'You want coffee?' I was standing on the coconut matting by the door, catching the pungent smell of cigarette ends dumped in a water glass container. 'The apprentice is here. He can make coffee,' he repeated as Eva came out from the chart room holding her rifle and waving it in my direction.

The wheelman kept his eyes straight ahead. 'Over here. Walk slow. I had no intention of doing, otherwise. 'Do as she says,' said Mr Thomson. 'Be quiet. We give orders. You are here to assist only,' snapped Pepe. Eva turned and jabbed me with the rifle as I entered the dimly lit chart room. Jane and Mr Jones the Radio Officer were on the day bed bound hand and foot. The Radio Officer was gagged. Jane wasn't.

Eva sat next to Jane, who looked relieved that she was not alone with her, but showed resignation in her face that the terrorists were now in total control. Eva held the gun in her right hand, barrel pointed towards me , while caressing Jane's hair and left cheek. 'Do not be upset mon cherie Eva is here. I so dislike tying you up, but Pepe he does not understand.' 'I do understand, 'Pepe called out. 'Leave the girl alone, she's not interested and I may have to kill her if you become emotionally attached.'

The matter of fact way this was said sent a chill down my back. Eva lent across and kissed Jane on the cheek, whilst watching the reaction from me. Jane trying unsuccessfully to avert her head to avoid the kiss. 'You like Jane, I see this,' said Eva. 'It is the best hostage for us. You all like Jane and I am captivated. Now it is difficult, but Jane will maybe leave with me.' The kidnap, I realized was more than just to control the ship, revealing also now a predatory reason for holding Jane captive. The Radio Officer hunched up in the corner of the settee, looked terrified, but Jane's was one of defiance. Head turned away, as Eva placed an arm over her shoulder, lightly lifting her hair and letting it fall. 'It is such a shame that I have to tie your arms, but I can stroke your pretty blond hair. Eva will protect you.' She again looked towards me as she started caressing Jane's neck, the intention no doubt to get a reaction from me. 'Don't do anything Mike, just do as they say,' Jane said calmly. 'They have no use for any of us, they just want to get the arms and ammunition off the ship. They live for their cause.'

'That is right, you understand so much for such a young woman. That is also what makes you so attractive to me. We can be partners together, lovers, but also look after each other in the fight for freedom. We will be so compatible.' 'Don't count on it. I'm not attracted to other women, in that way,' said Jane. 'We shall see, mon cherie, we shall see.' 'Eva,' Pepe called again from the wheelhouse. I was getting the impression that the ordering of Eva by Pepe was a front and she the more ruthless of the two in pursuit of her intent, ambition or passion. 'Eva,—EVA.' 'Yes, I am not deaf—only when I choose to be. What is it now?' 'You can unlock the Captain's cabin, after the coffee. He will need to be here when our boats arrive.' 'Si, si. Jane can come with me.' She lowered her voice to a whisper and reached out to caress Jane's arm. 'Do not worry mon cherie I will let you say goodbye to them before you leave with us on our boats.'

While sorting out the night tray of cups and saucers on the chart table, I listened to Pepe explaining to the Mate how the position of discharge for the crates of armaments was at Mar del Plato, in deep water, and in summer usually calm seas.

'I can teach you so many things,' said Eva to Jane sitting behind me. 'Your legs are right for dancer's legs.' I turned to see her holding Jane's ankle and running her hand up each leg in turn like a fancier might do to a horse before an auction. Jane must have read my thoughts and nodded her head from side to side, as if to say ignore what Eva's doing and don't let it get to you, particularly after she said, 'There is someone else who admires these legs, I believe.' I walked across to pick up the kettle on the deck at the side of the day bed.

'But all this it is for later,' she continued stroking Jane's face. 'It's possible like the nurse Christina you can stay with me, but as companion with more personal involvement.' That remark horrified and upset me more than the abuse just witnessed. I changed my mind in an instant to seeing the commandos boarding as a very positive development.

On the chart table was a chart of the entrance to the River Plate, showing Montevideo, Uruguay on one side and on the other Mar del Plato, Argentina. I heard Pepe say to the Mate. 'You have seen the result of foolishness by one of your crew. They need to follow my instructions or I will shoot from where I am on the bridge. We have the girl, but you have seen that we will shoot anyone who obstructs our plans. 'The ship's crew will cooperate,' said the Mate. 'You've explained that the five crates in number three 'tween deck are guns and high explosive. We do not want these on board. The ship will be impounded. The authorities holding us responsible. 'It is good that you and your Captain understand the situation fully,' I heard Pepe say, before shouting out. 'The coffee, I will have black with dos sugar. Eva be sure to watch the young apprentice, that he does not try anything.'

'I am watching Pepe. He will not while I am here with Jane.' Eva moved across to where the Radio Oficer was tied up, who flinched not knowing what was going to happen. She turned to face me, waving the rifle. 'Untie this,' she said pointing to the first aid bandage wrapped around his mouth. I placed the kettle on the chart room table. 'I need the bathroom,' were Sparky's first words. That most likely accounting in part for the pained expression on his face. 'Untie the ropes as well,' she said, having broken off from telling Jane how she could live with her in an apartment in Mar del Plato.

I undid first the cord around his ankles and then his wrists, which took several minutes. 'Fill the kettle now,' she said. When I returned Eva was standing with her back to the chart room table. I plugged the kettle in and she grabbed me by the arm. 'You may go to bathroom Radio Officer. Be back before kettle is boiled,' she said, opening the chart dividers and clamping them either side of my upper right arm. 'Or I make more than scratches on young amigo. The needle points of the dividers scratched my skin as she drew them back. I tried to pull my arm away. 'Comprende?' 'Si, si, senorita,' he replied, which hopefully meant that he could achieve her demand in the time allotted. 'Eva when you have finished that coffee you can take the girl and lock her in our cabin and bring Captain Anderson and senora Anderson to the bridge.' said Pepe.

'You have told me that,' said Eva. She looked toward Jane as if expecting sympathy for the plight of women working with men. Jane gave a grimacing smile, perhaps to humour Eva, relieving some of the tension. Sparks, luckily achieved a return before the kettle boiled, with Eva directing me then to retie the rope around his legs and hands. When I entered the wheelhouse with the coffee, the Mate said, 'What about our

Radio Officer?' Pepe just shrugged his shoulders saying, 'He is dangerous to our mission. He may contact other ships when we go, that is if we let him live.' I hoped Sparks did not hear this. He looked scared witless as it was.

# Chapter 32

# Approach to Rendezvous

The Radio Officer was still tied by his hands and feet, but not gagged as before. Eva had left with Jane still captive to raise Captain Anderson and Mrs Anderson. They would comply with the demand, seeing Jane at gun point. Pepe standing in the corner of the chartroom overlooking Mr Thompson, when I returned from washing out the mugs in the wash basin.

'Can I trust this position,' he said stubbing his finger on the chart. 'Yes, the Second obtained a star sight earlier which meant our position is accurate. The ship is on Stand By, we can stop when we sight your boats.' 'Si, si I am aware of all this,' he said, stamping his foot, impatiently, 'I need reduction in speed when we are within a few miles of this position, not when we sight my boats.' The sailor on the wheel was staring at the overhead giro compass as I entered with more coffee, followed by Pepe. 'There, place it on there,' said Pepe, pointing the barrel of the gun in the direction of the wheelhouse window ledge.

I noticed a black revolver handle jutting out from beneath his waistcoat as he turned towards me. A more powerful looking weapon than the silver pistol Eva shot the Electrician with. 'You Second Officer can leave,' he said withdrawing the revolver, holding it above his head, squatting and pointing the pistol at an imaginary assailant entering on the far side of the bridge in front of Charlie. The sudden aggressive stance no doubt intended to intimidate the both of us. Charlie started and stopped. 'Yes, it is good to be able to be able to practise and be at the ready. You may leave the wheelhouse now Second Officer.' He clicked the serrated edge of the safety catch off before placing the revolver in the corner of the wheelhouse to the side of the cup of coffee, keeping the AK 47 over his shoulder. 'Here light me a cigarette,' he said placing a pack of Pall Malls and lighter on the ledge next to the coffee. He picked up the revolver, pointed it in my direction and waved the barrel across to where the Mate was now standing affirming the course steered by the wheelman. I tapped the side of the packet allowing a cigarette to pop out. Placed it in my mouth. Flicked the wheel on the lighter and lit it before handing it to Pepe. 'Gracie. You see I take no chances. I can shoot whenever I wish. My hands are free. 'You may take over from the wheel person. I presume that is your job, now. 'Yes, right,' I said as if everything that happened was an everyday occurrence.

The wheelman, a middle aged sailor, who was previously dismissive of we apprentices, gave a friendly smile and said. 'She'll be all right, son, once we get rid of those crates.' He would have heard Pepe talking to Eva, but not what was said by Eva in the chart room. Pepe might not be able to stop Eva taking Jane with her, that was my worry. 'Just give the apprentice the course and go back to your cabin', said Pepe. 'The sailor stepped away from the wheel , not wanting to aggravate the situation. 'One nine five degrees and she's taking a degree or two port helm to steady on course. 'Okay son, then she's all yours.' He stepped from the raised wooden plinth behind the wheel as I grabbed hold of the uppermost brass capped hand hold indicating the rudder was in the mid- ships position.

It was surreal. The officer of the watch performed his duty, but in the corner of the wheelhouse was this malignant individual—Pepe. Although his name probably a pseudonym, as most likely was Eva's. He appeared to be the leader, but Eva was a persuasive force in all that happened. The Mate asked, 'Are you staying on the bridge for this watch? Or is your partner relieving you?' 'What is it to do with you. I decide what happens. We can choose to change places. I have slept earlier. I am refreshed. Eva has been on the bridge and now I await the arrival of our boats.' 'Yes I'm looking out for them,' said the Mate, binoculars scanning what I assumed to be the Argentinean coast on the starboard side, humouring Pepe by complying. 'We can go to half speed, now. It is better we approach the area more slowly.' The Mate rang the telegraph to half speed.

My eyes were now more accustomed to the gloom. Pepe opened the ammunition box at his feet. Should a shooting match begin, he would be well prepared. A daring but, so far well executed plan. Now we were well into Argentinean territorial waters. There were unlikely to be American or British warships nearby. The major concern for the ship was unlit fishing boats or local ferry traffic between coastal townships. A full moon escaped from clouds and gave a reflection across the water.

In the east the horizon was lightening. I needed somehow to attract the Mate's attention. The slowing of the ship might require more rudder usage to maintain the course of 195 degrees. I called out, looking across. 'Taking more steerage. Perhaps you need to see sir?' The Mate gave me a quizzical look, but removed the binoculars from his eyes letting them hang by their leather strap, before moving from the front of the wheel- house to stand by my side. Pepe glanced across, but it seemed routine and he looked back out to sea. Before calling out I slipped the White Ensign flag card on the glass of the giro compass repeater. The white expanse on the flag and the union jack clearly visible. I pointed to the giro. 'She's swinging a bit. Could it be the tidal flow?' I asked the Mate as he noticed the card. I turned the card and revealed the "Royal Navy Aboard" message. The Mate clearly understood and gave a thumb's up to acknowledge this. I pocketed the White Ensign. 'Nothing to worry about son. I can see you know what to do. More helm. Slower speed means things become

140

sluggish.' 'What's the difficulty?' asked Pepe. 'Nada,' said the Mate. 'It's perfectly normal. He is right to let me know what is happening. The slower speed is making the steering sluggish.'

# Chapter 33

# On Lookout

The engine room phone buzzed. 'Answer it,' snapped Pepe from the corner of the wheelhouse. The Mate walked to the wall mounted phone near to the chart room door. 'Hello—bridge,' said the Mate. There was a pause, then he spoke again. 'I see and for how long? Ten minutes?' The Mate cupped his hand around the phone. 'What do they say?' demanded Pepe. 'The engine room have a problem they want to stop the engine. They need to change the fuelling to diesel.' 'Why was this not mentioned before?' Said Pepe. 'Ten minutes, no more. The engine must be ready for when we are near to the boats.' 'Ten minutes—no more than ten, though Third,' he said before hooking the phone up. 'This, better be genuine, and not funny business,' said Pepe. 'This is standard procedure, going over to diesel for better manoeuvrability.' 'That's right,' I said, suddenly feeling the need to back the Mate up. He gave me a wide- eyed look, as if to say, 'Watch it, he may think something's up.' 'We're now in the zone I marked on the chart—si?' 'Yes we are,' said the Mate, who was inspecting a print out from the echo sounder on the port side of the wheelhouse. 'There's a discrepancy between this reading and the recorded depth on the chart.' 'By how much?' asked Pepe. 'About two fathoms,' said the Mate, but adjusting this figure. 'That's over four metres less.' 'The sand banks shift when there are storms I know this area well.' He went across to see the reading. 'It is static now. Still have plenty of water. But we are near. I need the funnel and deck lights to be switched on before the engine is ready. My boats need to see the ship.' 'I'll send the lad to do that, but I'll need the lookout from the Monkey Island.' 'That I will do,' said Pepe, un-shouldering his

AK 47 and flinging open the bridge door. He strode to the outer part of the bridge. There was a rattling of the fire arm's mechanism before he called out. 'Hey you, on Monkey Island come down to take the wheel, pronto.'

The sailor managed a strangulated, 'Yes, Senor Pepe, I'm on my way.' The name of the folk singing passenger no longer seemed suitable for this heavily armed terrorist. No longer the right form of address. It was probably the fastest time ever made from the Monkey Island and into the Wheelhouse by the sailor. 'The course is 195 degrees, 'I said—taking a few degrees starboard helm.' 'Okay, 195 it is, then,' he replied, as the giro compass clicked directly on to course. 'I want all lights on the front of here switched on. The ones to light the deck and also the funnel lights,' Pepe called out. 'Got that lad,' said the Mate, 'and when you return you can go on lookout.' 'Right, sir,' I said.

As I scrambled down the companionway I heard the loud buzz of the telegraph followed by the dying of the pulsating main engine as I entered the funnel to switch on the spot-lights. 'All right Mike?' I recognized Lieutenant Payne's voice. 'Shhh,' The voice continued. The only light inside the funnel came from the gridded barred area above the engine room, which stretched around the far side of the main exhaust manifold. There was washing, jeans and tee shirts pegged on a line across the grid. A hanging shirt was lifted and I recognized the blackened face of the Lieutenant. I also got a glimpse of wet- suited figures, backs against the funnel, guns trained over to where I was standing by the door. 'Where are they. Are they both on the bridge?' He whispered moving closer toward where I stood on the metal decking. 'No only Pepe. Eva's in the accommodation. They've both got AK47s and pistols. I've been told to switch on the funnel lights and mast deck lights on, and then go back on watch.' 'On lookout?' 'Yes,' 'That's good. We'll just hope we can get the woman

143

out on deck. We're placing smoke canisters in the passenger accommodation.

'You'd best get a move on or he might suspect something.'
'Right,' I said flicking the light switch for the funnel spotlights. I reopened the funnel door and slammed it shut behind me , re- aligning the top and bottom locking levers. I remembered thinking the smoke canisters could be a good way of getting Eva out on deck. I scrambled down two companionways to the embarkation deck and down the metal stairway leading to the main deck, hoping extra speed counteracted any delay. Lights from the accommodation shone on the ladder and rails leading to the foredeck. We were nearer to the shore than I'd known the ship to be out of normal shipping lanes. I felt more confidence in Lieutenant Payne's plan now that he said he was going to place smoke canisters in the passenger accommodation. Eva the queen bee could be smoked out of the accommodation by this revised plan. The building of an abandon ship scenario out of smoke exiting the engine room window, seemed a bit far- fetched.

# Chapter 34

# Boats Sighted

With the engine stopped I was more aware of the quiet on deck save for the lapping of water against the ship's side. The normal speed was fourteen knots. The momentum going forward, likely to continue for the ten minutes allotted for the switch to diesel. After encountering the Lieutenant and his men in the funnel I realized how precarious my situation was, if Pepe suspected me of not following his instructions properly. Questions asked, which might betray my being associated with a rescue. I felt more secure with the situation once both sets of mast head deck lights were switched on.

When I returned to the bridge the Mate was scanning the shoreward side with binoculars. 'You'll probably spot them first.' He was going to continue, but Pepe stepped out on to the starboard side of the bridge. 'Go on the top deck. Here take these.' He thrust the other set of binoculars into my hands before stretching an impatient hand toward the Mate, who handed over the set he was holding. 'They will be arriving from the shore side. Two long funnelled ships with towing platform barges.' The understanding and control Pepe showed over shipboard proceedings indicated a naval background. Although he was giving orders at this point my mind was not made up about whether he was more significant than Eva in the organization. On the Monkey Island I noticed that daylight was arriving. The lights were no longer visible from the shore. A puff of black smoke made me train the binoculars. I could see a tall funnel and a varnished wooden bridge structure. I yanked the copper cap off the voice pipe. 'Vessel about eighty degrees on the starboard bow, showing smoke from funnel.' It was 0700 hours—I looked aft and smoke

145

billowed out from the engine room sky lights. The funnel spot lights picked out the smoke effectively in the dawn light. Both Pepe and the Mate were out on the starboard side of the bridge. I shinned down the companionway on the port side. First I slipped the binoculars back in their holster. The wheelman's eyes were glued to the compass. I looked up and saw two rubber suited commandos crouched behind the door on the far side of the bridge. Both with index fingers raised to their lips requesting I did not give their presence away. 'White smoke exiting engine room skylights on port side,' I called out as I walked across the wheelhouse. The pre-arranged signal.

The engine room phone buzzed. I picked it up. 'Bridge speaking,' I said,—'Mike Peters, apprentice.' 'Mike, it's the Third,' came the reply. 'Where's senor Pepe?' 'Out on the bridge.' 'Have you reported the smoke from the skylights?' 'Yes, Third.' 'Call him to the phone. Say the Third Engineer needs to speak with Senor Pepe. Okay?—about a fire.' The Mate was now standing in the bridge doorway about to enter. I gave him the message. 'The Third Engineer needs to speak with Senor Pepe about a fire in the engine room.' Luckily he turned and relayed the message before seeing the commandos. 'Senor Pepe. The engine room needs to speak to you about a fire.' This had the desired effect of getting him back in to the wheelhouse. I held out the phone, while the Mate went to look at the compass heading. He said afterwards that it was just as well I'd informed him about the boarding party.

I'd probably given the game away by the look on my face seeing the commandos crouched there ready to pounce. Pepe never made it to the phone. The commandos threw him on to the coconut matting of the wheelhouse. The engine was on stop. The relative quiet broken by a bang of a door flung open on the deck below. I ran through the wheelhouse and out on to the bridge- portside. Eva was flat on the deck. Her shoulders held by a commando on each side. 'Colonial pigs. We fight for the freedom of Las Malvinos,' she screamed, but calmed down when a knife was placed against her throat. I ran down the companionway to help Jane, who was holding out her arms for the rope around her wrists to be cut by a commando before I arrived. 'You're safe now love,' the commando said as the ties fell away. 'Jane are you okay?' I said, reaching out my hands. 'Yes Mike. I'm okay now,' and smiled. A smile I'll never forget and then placed her hands on my shoulders. 'You were really brave Mike.' 'You were the brave one,' I said. 'I'd do anything for...' but at that moment Mrs Anderson who'd followed me down from the bridge put her arm around Jane. I turned away, because tears were streaming down my eyes. Relief at Jane's release. I watched as they tied Eva to one of the lifeboat davits. Her foul rant ended when Miss Devlin gave the commandos her scarf as a gag. Her brother Dennis stood coughing nearby. Both forced out on deck by the smoke. Miss Devlin seemed unaffected and was talking to the Lieutenant who'd unbuttoned the boiler suit he must have acquired from the Third Engineer. This revealed epaulettes on his tropical white shirt. I saw Mr Thompson signalling for me to return to the bridge. I acted instinctively and went down to help Jane, but without permission from the officer of the watch.

'Not supposed to leave your post, you know,' he said, as I stepped back on the bridge. Captain Anderson although ashen faced managed a smile. There were streaks of white in his hair I'd not noticed before and he looked older. On the other side I saw Pepe guarded by the commandos with hands tied. It was Mr Thomson who met the Lieutenant as he ran from the boat deck, up the companionway to the bridge. Captain Anderson went down to meet Jane who was walking with her mother towards the steps. He held her to him. She looked up, relief on her face. Her father the one most distressed. She managed a smile for me standing by the railing above. 'There was nothing you or anyone could do,' I heard her say. 'But I'm your father and you were taken away in front of me,' he said, coughing back tears. 'It's Leckie—that really upset me,' she said. 'How is he?' 'Mr Thompson has said he died, shortly afterwards.' 'That's terrible.' It was Jane who was doing the comforting. Mrs Anderson took control of the situation, at the foot of the companionway. 'Paul—Jane's all right. She's got some nasty marks on her arms and wrists, but nothings broken. We'll go into the wheelhouse. Christina's fetching some salve for the marks on her skin.' I admired the family for their courage, but also clearly understanding how devastating the effect must have been for Captain Anderson, powerless to help his daughter taken hostage at gunpoint. Mr Thompson turned to me and said, 'The Lieutenant's been telling me about your assistance. You certainly put me in the picture with the flag,' he said refering to the White Ensign. 'Clever people these Chinese,' said Lieutenant Payne, smiling at the both of us. Mr Thompson walked over to the companionway to greet Mrs Anderson and Jane as they arrived on the bridge. 'We'll sit in the Chart Room, and make a cup of tea, if that's all right,' said Mrs Anderson. 'Exactly what I was going to suggest.'

'Mike Peters,' he said. 'It's back to work for us. I want you to go on the wheel for now. I'd like to know more about what happened leading up to the rescue, but later.' It didn't seem over as I followed Jane and Mrs Anderson into the wheelhouse with two terrorists vessels approaching 'The Lieutenant said you were a key player in the rescue plan,' she said smiling and walking back in full view to kiss me on the cheek. I wished she hadn't, at the time, with the wheelman looking on.

I discovered afterwards that she knew more about the situation from the Lieutenant than those of us on the bridge. It was a kiss of gratitude. Looking back I realized she must have known how I felt about Jane. Jane dismissive about any feelings toward me other than a sister towards a brother. There was relief, that Jane and the Radio Officer, Mr Jones were free, and that Pepe and Eva were in the custody of the Royal Navy. That sense of relief did not last for me while the terrorist ships were closing in. The course was 079 degrees and we were heading away from the coast on slow ahead, when I took the wheel. 'You can return to the wheel at seven fifty before the changeover,' the Mate said to the sailor 'We still need a lookout.' 'Right Mr Mate, I'll get back on lookout.' A few minutes later his voice came out of the brass trumpet speaker above the wheel. 'Vessel seventy degrees on starboard bow. The Mate grabbed the binoculars and walked to that end of the wheelhouse. 'It's a warship approaching at speed,'—he called back to Captain Anderson and Lieutenant Payne as they entered the Wheelhouse. 'And what about these two?' said the Captain waving at the approaching terrorist vessels 'Are we in for a shooting match?' They were about a mile away—having steamed from the direction of Mar del Plato.

# Chapter 35

# Commander Geoff Hanbury Explains

'It's not as dire as it appears Captain,' replied the Lieutenant, calmly. 'Those vessels are in our hands. We boarded yesterday afternoon.' He went over to where the Mate was standing. 'That's Resolution coming in to assist,' he said. 'We'll just have to hope it's too early in the morning for the Argentineans to notice from the shore. We picked up radio signals, between these terrorist vessels, previously at anchor. One gave the latitude and longitude of the rendezvous and did not disguise the fact that they were meeting Albany Princess—your ship Captain. When we were informed the ship had been hijacked we decided to board and take their crews hostage. We kept them on station after the hijack of Albany Princess. It was not certain we could regain control before the rendezvous and then they murdered your Electrician.'

Lieutenant Payne called to one of the commandos. 'Jenkins take the prisoner down to the boat deck.' 'Right sir,' he called back from where he was standing on the bridge. 'You will be shot. My men have guns on the boats,' said Pepe, unaware of the situation on entering the wheelhouse. 'Your men are over there,' said the Lieutenant pointing to where the destroyer was approaching. 'We now control your boats, senor Pepe,' he said. 'Filthy colonialists , this will not stop us from taking back what belongs to Argentina.' 'This ship does not belong to you,' said Captain Anderson. Intimidation and threats will not further your cause. Now you will have to accept the consequences. 'Take him down to the boat deck Petty Officer,' said the Lieutenant, 'and tie him to the other side of the lifeboat. I'll be signalling for a launch to take them off.'

'But, Captain Anderson, sir, are you all right? It's been a horrific experience for you and your family.' 'We are now, thanks to you and your men, Lieutenant. There is much I don't understand, but I'm sure you'll update me,' 'Captain we boarded as you appreciate uninvited last night, from HMS Resolution.' 'A very welcome boarding Lieutenant, but how did you know we'd been hijacked?' 'We had an informant. I'll explain Captain—Chief.' He turned to Mr Thompson. 'That Aldis,' he said, pointing to the lamp dangling from a hook in the corner of the wheelhouse. 'May we use it?' 'There's a job for you,' said the Mate, pointing towards the lamp. For one terrifying moment I thought he was going to suggest I operated the Aldis lamp. 'Untie it and set it up,' he said. Lieutenant Payne walked over to the railings, and whistled to the deck below—'Signals need your skills up here to speak with Resolution.' At this point a white boiler suited figure—the Third Engineer strode up the companionway two steps at a time and on to the bridge. The Lieutenant stood aside to let him through, but stiffened to attention before announcing in the wheelhouse—'this is Commander Hanbury, from MI6.'

A look of bafflement came across Captain Anderson's face. 'Our Third Engineer, but,' 'I've some explaining to do,' said the previously Third Engineer, now a Commander. 'It goes back to Captain Smith's death. There is further distress, because Captain Smith didn't die of a heart attack. He was poisoned by Pepe who got aboard disguised as a customs officer, immediately after Albany Princess docked. Eva and Pepe, we believe kidnapped a customs officer after he left his house, forced his car into a layby, took his uniform and left him tied up on the back seat, covered by a blanket. Captain Smith was a threat to their operation. He would have recognized them since his mistress in Buenos Aires invited Eva and Pepe, as you know them, to dinner, a year ago. She is also a member of The Freedom

151

Fighters for Las Malvinos. No one else on the ship knew them, but Captain Smith would have recognized them.'

'An innocent bystander, all the same I'd say,' said Captain Anderson. 'Yes that is true Captain. They murdered him when the ship docked last August to prevent their identity being revealed when registering as passengers. A later post-mortem revealed the cause of death as cardiac arrest due to acute poisoning. The customs officer's uniform was recovered from a waste bin. Carelessly a signed programme from their last concert had been left in the inside pocket of the jacket.'

The Lieutenant interrupted this explanation. 'We're alert-ing our forces that the merchantman is freed Commander, if that's okay and then getting a pinnace over from Resolution.' 'Go ahead Lieutenant. We need to get a move on before Argentina wakes up to our being here,' said the Commander. Immediately the Aldis started clicking out a message to the former terrorist vessels. Commander Hanbury continued explaining the events leading up to the hijack. 'My depart-ment decided to get me on board, but it was then believed there was Russian involvement and arms were for the exist-ing Argentinean government. We even thought Pepe was a Russian agent at this point.

I replaced your previous Third, when it became apparent that the cargo was switched in Liverpool. A Russian ship, that docked earlier discharged five crates, which were traced to the warehouse supplying cargo to Albany Princess—your ship—Captain. There was deception taking place. The crates were labelled for Buenos Aires, but with assistance from Uruguay, we intended to intercept them at Montevideo. The Resolution was tasked to shadow your ship once in the South Atlantic and I first made radio contact just south of the Equator.

I witnessed Jane being taken hostage in the smoke room, but I very much regret having to say we never realized they'd planned this earlier. We knew they most likely murdered

Captain Smith, but were not expecting such a brutal takeover of your ship. 'Your department and me together,' said Captain Anderson. 'They were under suspicion as passengers, but we had no evidence that they were a direct threat to your ship. We believe now that they could be part of a splinter group seeking to overthrow the present regime. That still may be true. The Foreign Office have been researching their backgrounds after the hijack yesterday evening. You, may recall my late arrival on board Captain Anderson just before sailing.' I certainly did, even if the Captain didn't, as I spun the wheel trying to keep the compass reading on 079 degrees.

'The long and the short of it is that we contacted your company to facilitate my presence on board. We didn't for see the possibility of a hijack, but were planning to inter-cept when in Uruguayan waters, not before. 'I see,' said the Captain. 'Well I'm not sure I do Commander, but go on'. 'Customs officials boarded the Russian ship in Liverpool on the pretext of looking for drugs and took hold of the ship's manifesto. It was only after you sailed that it was known the crates contained arms and ammunition. There's a consign-ment of whisky going to the Russian embassy, and our intel-ligence branch believed the crates were for Buenos Aires, as part of this consignment. Resolution planned to contact you and request to come aboard.'

'By the way Lieutenant I take it your Gunnery and Bomb Disposal Unit are on these captured tug boats?' 'Correct, Commander,' replied Lieutenant Payne. A sailor returned to take over from me on the wheel as the Mate ordered. It was seven fifty.

'I need to signal Commander for a launch to take off the prisoners,' he said. 'You carry on Lieutenant. We can then inspect these crates, and remove them. I'm sure Captain Anderson understands the need to get things moving before attracting attention from the Argentine military in the area.'

'It suits me moving away from this sand banked coastline. Getting rid of illicit armaments on board another plus. Mr Thomson get the Bosun to raise the derricks next to Number Three Hold, will you?' The Bosun was standing on the bridge viewing the activity on board the destroyer close by. 'I'll get him on to it straightaway,' said the Mate leaving the wheelhouse to instruct the Bosun.

'You were saying Commander.' 'Yes, Captain. The hijack took us by surprise. The Resolution was only by luck here in position ahead of your new course line, when it met up with the two largish tugs with towing pontoons intercepting radio messages about removing crates from Albany Princess. A decision was made to board them. I was informed of the tugs connection after meeting up with the Lieutenant.' 'We're part of a secret service operation, then,' said Captain Anderson. 'I prefer reading about this type of event in an Ian Fleming novel, not having my daughter taken hostage in a terrorist operation, like this.' The signals officer having contacted the a approaching former terrorist vessels moved to the far side of the bridge to signal HMS Resolution. I assisted unwinding the flex from the plug extending the Aldis lamp's reach. I recognized the "double A Morse" call up sign and "Merchantman secured," but it all got too fast for me after that. The Lieutenant dictated the message out of hearing on the far side of the bridge.

My earlier feeling that the Commander was no everyday shipboard engineer on target. 'You can get breakfast,' said the Mate, as I crossed the wheelhouse floor'—after you've got that mate of yours up.' I realized then that Tom knew nothing of the rescue. Stepping down the companionway from the bridge I noticed the eight to twelve sailor make a face, as he walked past the terrorists tied to the lifeboat davits at bow and stern. He wouldn't have dared do that earlier. 'I didn't care for their singing that much anyway,' he said, as if tying them up was somehow the result of their singing not the hijack.

# Chapter 36

# Waking Tom

The sailors from HMS Resolution were stood at ease in drill formation outside the funnel as I passed them on the boat deck. There was a thumbs up and a smile from a couple of them. An incredible chain of events had occurred in just over twelve hours. I considered how dire things could have been, if the Navy hadn't listened to the tug boats radio conversation earlier and decided to board them. I walked down the companionway to the accompaniment of the clatter from the derricks being raised by Number Three hatch and went into the accommodation through the storm door on our deck.

'Tom shake a leg,' I called out after knocking on his cabin door. I opened it. 'It's over the ship's been taken back.' Tom sat bolt upright in his bunk. This time I sensed he was fully awake. 'What do you mean?' 'Just that,' I said, as Tom rubbed his eyes to accustom himself to the light streaming in the open door. 'How's it been taken back, not by you?' Momentarily, I considered saying yes, but decided I'd better tell the truth. 'The Navy have been tracking us and boarded this morning. I got woken by a tapping on my port hole. It was as well they choose my porthole. I doubt whether they'd woken you,' I said.

'That they would.' Tom never admitted he was a heavy sleeper. I didn't pursue it. 'And I slept through all this.' 'The ship did. The boarding party hid in the funnel and then created an alarm. 'And I slept through all of this,' Tom said in disbelief again. A deck hand framed the door space to Tom's cabin. 'The Mate says you two are to come on deck immediately before breakfast and assist with the unloading of the crates. 'What crates?' Asked Tom. 'Best ask the Navy they're running the show.' He turned to go, but came back. 'The Mate's at number three hatch,' he said before leaving, again.

'We've crates of ammunition and guns stowed on board. I'll fill you in about what's happened as you get ready,' I said to Tom, who was now very much awake. Within ten minutes we were out on deck. I saw the Mate on the main deck when I looked down from above. One tug boat was no more than thirty feet away from the side. We were moving slowly seawards. Sporadic firing of the main engine taking place, to maintain some forward momentum. A heavy lift derrick was now plumbed over Number Three hold, another over the ship's side. The two wires shackled to the lifting hook and the pontoon behind the tug, perhaps twenty feet from the ship's side Two deckhands stood holding lines to throw to the waiting Royal Navy sailors on board. The Bosun was in the driver's seat at Number Two testing that power was on. Both two and three winches being needed to pull the pontoon alongside with ship's ropes. I missed the white boiler suited figure of Leckie, who would have been standing nearby, checking on how the electric winches were performing. 'You two can assist getting the lines away and then securing the ropes,' said the Mate. Both of us took a look down the hold. The side of one crate now opened revealed double racks of AK 47s; another with machine guns on a tripod arrangement, with wires holding them secure within the crate. Chippy was down there with the Navy, claw hammer in hand, helping with the opening of the crates.

'There's no explosive risk here, Mr Mate,' the gunnery inspecting officer called up. A rapid clatter of footsteps came from mid-ships. Five sailors fanned out on deck, holding machine guns, positioning themselves behind winches—out of sight. The Lieutenant followed. 'It might be best if your hands secure the lifting wires. I've just heard a plane has been spotted by Resolution. We don't know if it's military. It may not be anything to do with this, but my men will be ordered to fire, if we're threatened,' he said.

'We can manage the lifting of the crates, can't we Bosun?' said the Mate. 'We can that Mr Mate,' he said, as if this activity was an everyday event for him. 'Lieutenant we'll have these crates up and over in no time at all, by Jez. That's if Chippy knows how to nail them together again.' Chippy heard the Bosun. 'They'll be better than new Mr Mate—you watch Mr Mate—Lieutenant.' There was a twirling sound followed by another as lines were thrown to the pontoon. Tom and I split up to assist with the ropes being lowered. Then holding them to wrap them around the winches to pull the platform alongside. There were five large crates to discharge with metal ringbolts on top. A wire cradle like harness was shackled on to the crates before being lifted on deck. The second pontoon was attached alongside the first. The crates lowered on to each in turn. When loaded they were set adrift and picked up by the waiting tugs.

Pepe and Eva were made to stand by the gangway. Incongruously Wann descended from the deck above with a tray of coffee and biscuits. The armed guard released Eva and Pepe's ties and Pepe was allowed a cigarette with his coffee. It all seemed far too civil, I remembered thinking at the time, after the mayhem they'd caused. The plane failed to appear, but a barge from Resolution drew alongside. With a polished looking hull, brass cleats shining and scrubbed white deck planking. The coxswain with a white holstered pistol belted around his waist. A rating ran up the gangway with lifejackets, when alongside, which Pepe and Eva would be made to wear before being escorted down.

My thoughts were interrupted by the Mate, as I looked at the barge alongside. He said to Tom. 'You can get your breakfast now. They may be waiting awhile for their belongings to be packed. Once the terrorists and crates are removed we'll be making for Montevideo. Then you can assist Chippy with unbolting the locking bars on the hatches and checking out the rat guards.' 'Right Chief,' said Tom. First Mates can be depended on to not let anything out of the ordinary interfere with their shipboard routine, where possible. Mr Thompson was no exception. The hijack was like a fire now extinguished and it was back to normal shipboard routine, so to speak.

# Chapter 37

# Arrival at Montevideo

'Amigo, amigo, AMIGO.' The voice came up from the dock below. I was on the foredeck with the line to throw ashore. The end was weighted. A monkey's fist worked with three strands of line around what looked like a large black pebble. The black just visible through the strands weaved round it. It was like swinging a yoyo, but you needed to be sure there was a clear run of line to take it and the fist clear of the gap between ship and quay. Those on the jetty making sure they didn't get thumped by the heavy projectile as it landed.

This time the line fell across the concrete dock. My caller, about fifteen with jet black hair wearing washed out blue overalls. He smiled back, and ran to grab hold , before it slipped away, wrapping it around a bollard. Shipboard the end was already tied to the rope loop on the far side of the railings, ready for release shore wards. Two wharf men started pulling on the line. The rope on deck uncoiled like some bulky snake descending from a tree.

Slowly at first assisted by the two sailors, then it gathered momentum of its own, before it dropped down between ship and quay wall. They hauled the loop along the quay and back to the bollard. Once over the bollard—back on board, the rope was turned twice around the winch. A reversing of the ship's engine stopped forward movement though the ship was still away from the dock wall. Tension developed in the rope from the winch hauling in slack.

Eventually wire rope springs at each end would hold Albany Princess alongside in a scissor grip, together with ropes; some of which would appear to sag before reaching the bollards suggesting they were surplus to requirements—but extra shore-lines were invaluable should a Pampero (fierce tornado like wind) hit the dock area.

I was previously sent down to assist the Mate, from the bridge. After lunch in the afternoon. Following the hijack Jane was with Charlie, the Second Mate on the bridge assisting with the upgrading of charts. Christina suggested to Mrs Anderson that, although Jane experienced the trauma of being tied up in the chart room it might be a good idea to go back there to regain confidence. It being similar to getting back on a horse after being thrown. Jane told me about this later.

After reporting to the Mate in the wheelhouse that day at four I met up with Jane in the chartroom. 'You were so courageous, like a protective brother Mike, she said. 'Especially when Eva threatened you with these.' She walked the long pointed brass handled dividers, across the chart, to measure the width of the River Plate's estuary.

I went over to the table. 'I never knew it had such a wide river entrance,' she said. 'I've heard it said that it's the world's widest river mouth,' I remember saying.

As I stood on the foredeck the memory of the hijack experience I remember came back with a chilling intensity. It is in life and death situations when you get to you realize what matters. Protective love and romantic hope joined forces at this point. In the instant when I saw Jane tied up on the day bed, I was terrified, but my mind worked overtime to make it look as if I knew nothing about the Royal Navy being on board. It was a great relief to see that Jane was relaxed and able to talk about the experience. Nothing else mattered.

It was a compliment, but a disappointment. Like when a girlfriend says she really likes you and still sees you as a best friend after ditching you for someone else. In a sense the rescue emphasised the fact that my love for Jane could be seen by onlookers as a crush. Like a student has for a favourite teacher or for Jane—the beautiful princess discovering that her rescuer on the white charger is not a gallant stranger, but her younger brother. That was how I felt at the time.

A wheelman was kept on, which allowed Jane to practise steering the ship. The Second Mate full of praise to her dad for how quickly she acquired the skill. 'The crawler, telling the old man how good Jane was on the wheel,' was how Tom put it.—'The line, the line,' the Mate shouted out to the wharf men. The one who called "amigo" to me, untied the end from the rope. Once coiled he separated a good length and let it fall to the ground, before swinging and letting go the monkey's fist. As the line crossed the top railing he made a whip cracking arm movement, flexing the rope, causing the monkey's fist to wrap several times around the railing. A skill which may have been acquired rounding up cattle. Certainly more adept than my rudimentary rope throwing technique. I glanced up to see Jane, no longer on the wheel, but watching proceedings from the port side of the bridge. The ship was being eased closer to the dockside, by ropes fore and aft. Understandably, there was concern that the trauma effect of the hijack might lead to flashbacks. Just then, she seemed absorbed in watching proceedings. It was really only then that I realized how badly wrong the rescue by the commandos could have gone.

'Assist by the winch,' called the Mate from the f'o'c'sl'e. This entailed holding the rope as it was winched back aboard and coiled on deck. Chippy walked around Number One hatch knocking out wedges with his claw hammer. The Mate came down from the f'o'c'sl'e' deck, once the ship was securely alongside. Within half an hour several ropes were run out to the shore and the foredeck wire spring secured, running aft to pinch the ship into the jetty. The Mate satisfied with the work gave me instructions. 'Once the rat guards are in place and the life boats covered you and your mate can call it a day.' 'Right sir,' I said.

I was carrying the rat guards on to the fo'c'sl'e when an old Mercedes hearse arrived at the gangway. The Chief Steward went to meet the driver. There was some discussion before a coffin was removed from the back of the hearse by two other black suited men from the car. The horror of the murder came back to me, slowing me down from the task in hand. I heard the slow rattle of feet on the gangway as they carried the coffin to the embarkation deck. They took it into the Seaman's Mess room, where we knew Leckie's body had been temporarily placed ready for taking ashore. Within fifteen minutes the hearse was gone.

Tom arrived on the f'o'c'sl'e, while I was lashing a rat guard around the wire spring on the foredeck. His first remark was 'You're slow. The rats could have been on board while you've been fixing the guards.' 'Did you see the hearse taking Leckie away?' 'Yes, but it didn't stop me getting the job done.' The sheer rise of the f'o'c'sl'e deck made it more tricky leaning over to clamp on rat guards than at the stern.

I was about to point this out to Tom, while he leant back on the railing, cigarette discreetly hidden in his left hand, not to advertise his smoking to the bridge, when Christina and Jane appeared. I could only imagine that they prepared in advance for going ashore, both now in black skirts. Jane was wearing a blazer like blue jacket. Christina a type of velvet waistcoat over a blouse. Ringlets of hair curling over both their shoulders, indicating probably a night spent in curlers. Light blue make up around the eyes. Christina's lipstick was a more vibrant pink, than Jane's, I recall.

'Heck you didn't waste any time getting out of work clothes,' said Tom. Christina and Tom had fallen out before the hijack. I was pretty sure Christina got to know about Rosa from Jane. Anything one was told would eventually get back to the other. 'We're going ashore with mother and father. We've been invited to visit the agent and his wife for a meal,' said Jane. 'I'm looking forward to a change of scenery.' 'It's all right for you Tom you weren't the one taken hostage,'

162

said Christina and you'll soon be meeting up with Rosa,' she added. 'There was the shooting,' 'Yes I was there, remember?' 'Stop squabbling,' said Jane.

Nerves were still frayed from the hijack and Jane who suffered the most seemed to be calmest of all. 'We're hoping to get away to go to the Mission aren't we Chris. The Chief Steward said it's in the same street. Father's given it the okay, but only because Charlie and the Fourth Engineer have said they'll definitely be there.' 'I only go to the Mission as a last resort,' said Tom, which was untrue. 'Does that make us a last resort,' retorted Christina. 'You know what I mean. It's like being at a church hall fete with the vicar organizing everything and everyone. 'We might see you later then,' said Jane, smiling. I looked across and nodded.

It was a cheap night out, which as apprentices we needed to consider. There was Buenos Aires ahead and a few good subs could put paid to three months wages. There was a whistle from farther down the main deck. I looked up and saw the Bosun, hand raised and pointing back and forth. Natalia Anderson was standing on the mid deck accommodation waiting to go ashore. Christina and Jane half turned and Jane waved to her mother as they walked back down the main deck. At the time, unconsciously we all attempted to move away from the horror of Eva and Pepe and how duplicitous their role had been.

'Once the boats are covered the Mate said we can finish for the day.' I said. 'Now you tell me. We could've finished that now and be going ashore, if you'd got a shift on—not wasted time chatting,' said Tom. 'That's rich coming from you,' 'Any way race you to the port lifeboat,' said Tom already standing by Number Two hold.

We showered and changed before going in to the saloon. Wann asked about where we were going. 'The Mission probably,' I said. 'Christina and Jane they also...' 'How do you know such top secret information Wann?' Asked Tom. 'No top secret. It was a deal that they went to agents only if they could go to Mission afterwards. Early I serve tea and—not like Chinese child Miss Jane made deal. She would go only if afterward they could escape from parents. Captain Anderson he ask Second Mate if he go to Mission. He said yes, and everything how you say "hunky dory." Chinese daughter would not make deals with father. She would follow instructions.' 'It must be very difficult for you Wann being such a "goody two shoes." How you survive on a British ship heaven only knows,' said Tom. 'Who is "goody two shoes?"' Asked Wann. 'Someone who never does anything wrong,' said Tom. 'That is not true, the Chief Steward he would disagree. He "goody two shoes." He gets cross and then he say, I am the cross he has to bear.' Wann held out the menu in front of Tom and looked enquiringly at me. 'Mr Mike you go to Mission?' 'Is that a question Wann?' He, just smiled. 'I'll have the baked cod with sauce,' said Tom. 'Same for me Wann.'

# Chapter 38

# Lift to the Mission

I noticed the grain dust was everywhere on deck. A camouflage blotting out colour, settled like snow on railings, portholes, and clinging to grime on the white paint of the accommodation. Around the hatches and on the ledges in the alleys, caught in the protective strips over the lights. Portholes were shut to keep out the heat and allow the air conditioning to fight the temperature down. The dust crept inside when doors were opened, from shoes and clothing. It gave off a dank smell. The grain itself lacked the golden glow that came from premium corn and barley, as I watched it plunge down the loading pipes. Rumour was that even the dirty dust in the holds could be used—washed and re-constituted into breakfast cereals.

It was seven thirty by the time we were both ready to go ashore. It coincided with the Second Steward's girlfriend arriving in her Pontiac. He went down the gangway to meet her, where she was parked just inside the dock gates. 'Just our luck she won't be going near the Mission,' said Tom. He was not at all upbeat about going ashore. 'How did Christina get to know about Rosa anyhow? You must have told her?' 'I didn't. Mr Thompson was telling Jane about how he looked forward to docking in Buenos Aires rather than Liverpool, because his fiancé lived there. Then he turned to me and said. I expect it's the same for your mate Tom when he arrives at Rosario. His girlfriend Rosa has an easy name to remember.' 'Jane would have heard.' 'Great,' said Tom. 'And then, she told Christina no doubt.' 'There was nothing I could do about that Tom!' 'And Father's home. He'll be wanting to know where I'm with studies. Looks like a fun time.'

With passengers, plus Jane and Christina on board, there had been distraction from study not including the hijack. Christina's relationship with Tom had cooled not unsurprisingly, when she discovered from Jane, that he already had a girlfriend in Rosario. On the ship's previous visit Tom's father came aboard and gave Tom instructions as to where he expected him to be in his course work. I knew Tom was not on target.

Chris Parkin the Second Steward waved to indicate that it was all right for us to hitch a lift. Tom was looking over the after deck, foot on rail, smoking a cigarette. 'It's okay Tom, we've got a lift,' I called out. 'Thank goodness for that, I was beginning to think we'd never get there tonight.'

It was a '53 Pontiac with American fins. We nearly disappeared in the backseats. Heads just about clear enough to see through the side windows. The Second's girlfriend was retouching her lipstick in the driving mirror, when we got in. Popped the tube into her handbag and leant across, avoiding the Second's lips, but giving him a rapid light kiss on his cheek. 'You never write Christopher. I write, but you do not reply.' Her black hair dangled in a ponytail tied with a bright red ribbon, in front of where I was sitting. The temptation to grab hold hard to resist, particularly when it skipped back and forth as she turned to talk to Chris. The pink lipstick fighting to exert itself against the deep red of her actual lips, as she spoke. I imagined the lipstick might be called Honey pink, for some reason. There was a hint of garlic and vino on her breath, but decided it complemented the musky scent of her perfume and freshly applied lipstick. I could get to love the smell of garlic and vino on a dark haired beauty like that, I was thinking, as I sat in the back listening to Chris getting a dressing down. She slipped the automatic lever forward, released the brake, and waved at the gateman on the way out. 'I did write as soon as we docked last time in the UK, but it must have been delayed.' 'I not believe you.' 'It was very interesting to read about your Arab stallion and how you are training it,' said Chris, trying to get on to safer ground, as she accelerated along the dock road towards the town. 'There's a horse for you this time. I take you for lesson tomorrow. You say you have afternoon free, Yes?' 'Yes, Natasha. I'm looking forward to that.' Liar I said to myself as we sped along the cobbled road. Chris mentioned that his Montevideo girlfriend was keen on horses. On previous visits horse riding had been avoided. It looked like on this visit she was going to get him on a horse. 'I'm okay with that Natasha,' said Chris.

'First tonight I have to see to the horses before everything else.' She smiled across at Chris, who looked suddenly more relaxed, at the mention of everything else. 'Your amigos. Where you say you go—the Mission? Natasha take you right outside. I met Christopher there. Is that not so?' Perhaps you also meet girls.' 'They're going to meet two English girls from the ship.' 'You no like girls in Montevideo then? Are we not pretty enough for you—eh?' She was teasing us. Tom was certainly more alive than before we left the ship. He chatted in Spanish to Natasha about how he thought Montevideo girls were prettier than Argentinean girls and wished we were staying longer than three days. That's what he told me afterwards. In fact they never stopped talking rapidly until we stopped outside the Mission. Chris no doubt wishing Tom was not in the car. 'Perhaps we come back later in car Christopher,' she said as we got out by the Mission. Chris nodded his head repeatedly saying no Natasha—not tonight, which could have been interpreted differently and not about visiting the Mission. Tom was in an expansive mood when we went through the Mission door. He may have fallen out with Christina , but not the whole of the female race as his chat with Natasha confirmed.

The Mission was a three story building. The recreational area was on the third floor. There was a large wooden cross in

167

the hallway. Red worn stair carpets. The stairway walls home to chipped gold framed pictures of the apostles. On the third floor a large porcelain figurine of Our Lady with vases of flowers on either side. The three doors were signed Chaplain's Office, Chaplain's Quarters and Meeting Rooms. Tom led the way. This was my first visit, but Tom confidently opened the door to the Meeting Rooms. This led to a small reception room with a desk. 'This is Mike, Sister Agnes.' 'Tom, you've found us again. What a nice surprise.' She smiled at me, but it was Tom who kept her attention. A slim silver haired woman, hair visible either side of a white and grey wimple, similar to that of a nursing sister. 'Pleased to meet you , to be sure. Father was asking about you. He was aboard your ship when it docked. You are lucky there are two English girls visiting tonight. It's so nice to hear English being spoken in a way that is natural.

# Chapter 39

# New Discovery Concerning Jane and Christina

The Meeting Hall was a large rectangular room with a blue curtained stage at one end tubular chairs stacked in front. By the door a semi-circular bar with armchairs and tables at the front. It was now nine o'clock. Two of the tables were occupied and other people were sat on bar stalls. 'There's no one from Albany Princess here,' I said to Tom. 'Not here,' he replied. Set midway down the opposite wall was a door with a faded gold varnished sign, which said Games Room. Tom went to open the door. 'There here Charlie,' it was the Fourth, Bill Mackay and Charlie the Second Mate. Bill looked across from where he held a dart pointed at the board. Charlie the far end with a piece of chalk in his hand.

Jane and Christina were playing table tennis in the far right corner. An attractive dark haired girl in a white skirt and pink top with a glass of coke, sat watching play. Jane waved her table tennis bat. Christina turned to see who she was waving at, but looked away quickly when she saw it was Tom. This didn't go unnoticed by the girl, who smiled, as if amused. 'We're going for a drink, you can have these if you want,' she said to Tom. 'We'll come with you.' Not sure that was what Christina intended. 'Like flies round a honey pot,' I heard Bill say to Charlie, chalking up his score. 'You're not to go outside the building,' Charlie said. 'I'm answerable to your mum and dad, Jane. Raymonde stay with them and let me know what's happening.' 'Si, Segunda Official, muy bueno.' The girl got up from her chair and curtseyed. Christina could not resist giving a curtsey as she passed by the Second Mate, repeating 'Si Segunda Official, muy bueno' Raymonde sat near to us on a bar stool and smiled invitingly, when we were in the Meeting Hall. There was some Argentinean beer, but we decided to pass on that. Raymonde already had a drink She was about my age.

'We'll get our own, you can get yours,' said Christina, turning away from Tom as she spoke. Jane gave me a look that said mind what you say. Raymonde smiled again, obviously still amused by the frisson between the two of them. Her eyes were an expressive blue, which contrasted with her olive skin and dark hair. I hoped she could speak some English, she was entrancing just to look at. The Padre entered. He was dressed casually in a blue jumper and grey trousers, but still with his dog collar. 'So nice to have a group from the Albany Princess here. You have shared a traumatic experience. Is one of you Jane? 'How did you know padre?' Asked Tom. Christina and Jane were sitting at the other end of the bar. 'I boarded your ship earlier, but I must have missed you. I spoke with Raymonde. She was excited about our visitors when she first got here.' He looked across to where Raymonde was sat drinking coke. 'Let me guess. 'He walked towards Jane and Christina. 'Raymonde told Sister Agnes she wished her hair was like Jane's. That suggests possibly the fairer one of you two young ladies, because I think it is not unusual for young women to complain about their hair being the wrong colour.

'Yes, it's me,' said Jane. 'I'm thinking of dyeing it black after being picked out by Pepe,' 'No, no senorita your hair is muy buena,' said Raymode turning towards Jane. The Padre continued speaking. 'I should admit I already know quite a bit about what happened. Two sailors from your ship were here earlier. It has not been reported in the news, but then maybe the authorities do not want it known. My colleague, Father Antonio in Buenos Aires has said they're not happy with the political situation. There is shouting about Las Malvinas. He knows that there must be economic problems—Tom how are you now. Not corresponding with the Communist Party, I hope.' Then I remembered Tom said he told the Padre on a previous visit that when in Russia on an ore carrier he was invited to join the Communist Party. He knew the padre would bite and talk about the evils of communism. He was not disappointed. 'You didn't keep those Party pamphlets did you?' I could have assured the Padre that they would have gone in the bin in the same way his Aunt Hilda's scripture tracts did.

'Dos coca cola, por favour,' Christina said to the Uruguayan bar girl. Jane had discovered a record collection at the side of the bar, next to an HMV record player. 'Christina there's a Buddy Holly album,' she said. The Padre broke off from talking to Tom.

'The player just needs plugging in. I'll set it up for you. I'm a fan. Such a tragedy, but the songs live on,' he said. Jane and Christina left their drinks at the table and danced to the music. Tom was in conversation with the Padre, so I plucked up courage and asked Raymonde if she would like to dance. 'If you like,' she said, and placed her Coke down before spinning around to face me and sliding off the high bar stool.

Every day was the song just beginning as I took her hand. Several other visitors to the Mission gathered around to watch us dancing. Raymonde was very pretty, but the words of the song about love coming my way were appropriate to how I felt about Jane, although unreciprocated. Self-conscious that I might look at Jane the way I did when dancing with Christina at the Electric Hall, while I held Raymonde's hand. 'Where we go?' she asked. 'Nowhere,' I said, just away from the bar. Raymonde, I considered, wasn't to know how I felt about Jane. She moved closer as we danced—she wanted to talk.

'I like to be Jane. The one who is Captain's daughter, si?' 'Si, 'You speak Spanish?' 'Muy poco,' I said. 'Okay, but my English no muy bueno,' she replied. 'No importante eres muy bella,' I said. 'Maybe, but you say that to all senoritas perhaps I think, si? You say that to Senorita Jane, Perhaps—I believe also,' Raymonde said raising her hands, finger clicking above her head. I must have blushed, because she laughed. 'I see things,' She said, lowering her hands and pointing toward her eyes. 'I see how you look at Senorita Jane. Only woman see these things, maybe. Although only my age she was perceptive—embarrassingly so. 'Enough dance, perhaps?' she said, as the song ended. 'Do you work at the mission?' I asked before we returned to the bar area. 'Sometimes, but Senora Anderson she ask if I go with Jane and Christina to mission. I work for senor Alfonso and Carolina. He is ship agent. Comprende?' 'Si, si,' I said. It explained how she already knew about Jane from the visit to the shipping agent's home. Jane and Christina came and sat with us after they finished dancing. It was then that Raymonde, said 'I would like very much to fly to England.' To which Jane replied, 'I wish I could stay here longer,'—'It's not our choice, but we have to leave South America, Raymonde,—because the British Foreign Service say we are at risk after the hijack. 'You never told us,' I said, not being able to help myself. 'We were only told an hour ago ourselves.' 'Mr machismo will be delighted,' said Christina, still simmering over Tom not telling her about Rosa his girlfriend in Rosario or because he had admitted to it now. It was difficult to work out either way.

The Buddy Holly record finished playing. The Padre came across to turn it over and Tom re- joined us. It could have been fraught with Christiana and Tom, but luckily Bill, the fourth engineer came across from the games room to suggest we make up two darts teams. Conveniently Tom and Christina ended up on opposing teams. I asked Jane why she thought they couldn't stay on the ship. 'Alfonso, the agent said Eva and Pepe were released by the Uruguayan authorities and put on a hydrofoil for Buenos Aires. Father got angry, because

172

he sees them as criminals. Alfonso said that it was all to do with diplomacy. That there may be a change of government in Argentina. I thought it funny, because of the way he said it'—'they were—Capitian Anderson—political hot potatoes for our little country.'

'I bet your mum and dad didn't think it was funny.' 'Let's forget about it Mike.'

'Mike, throw a dart, for Christ's sakes, said Tom. 'Jane's on our team—Jane—stop talking to the opposition.' Raymonde chalked up the score assisted by Bill. Charlie, Bill, Jane and Christina left in a taxi at ten o'clock for the ship. Tom chatted to the bar maid, a friend of Raymonde's, which led us to walk both of them back to their homes when the mission closed. Raymonde, kissed me on the cheek , and whispered mischievously. 'Perhaps the next kiss you make with senorita Jane?' 'I don't think so Raymonde,' I said, before we caught the bus back to the ship.

# Chapter 40

# Sud Dock Buenos Aires

Four single decker buses, crates containing machinery, a thousand bags of China clay, and drums of ethanol on the after deck were unloaded at Montevideo. The normality of being in port seemed strange after what we'd been through. We left on Friday morning for Buenos Aires, having docked the previous Tuesday. The small parcel of cargo for Montevideo meant a ship rarely stayed for more than a few days.

The water a murky brown as we travelled across the mouth of the River Plate past the skeletal like remains of the Graf Spey. The scuttled German capital ship from World War Two. There was plenty of arm waving and megaphone performance from the Pilot directed at the tugs, who seemed quite able to nudge the ship alongside unaided by any of the Pilot's theatrics.

Momentary quite ensued once alongside. The river tugs, chugged by, towing four or five barges, deeply laden. The water licking almost over their sides, giving an impression of defying Archimedes Principle. The stench of garlic, mixed with vino on the breath of stevedores. The Argentinean tobacco, more pungent than that of British. The cavalier handling of deck equipment might suggest to outsiders they owned the ship. A perforated metal tractor seat between two levers allowed the operator to sit or else stand, when agitated—which was nearly always.

One derrick over the hold, the other above a lorry on the quay. The operator's eyes darted downward into the hold, then ashore. This interspersed with aggressive throwing of the levers fully back or forward. A pretence perhaps of being the racing driver Juan Fangio on the race track. Cargo swinging up and on to waiting lorries. Wire zinging taut, while heavy crates and steel plate boxes were taken from below decks.

Lifting gear, victim to the temperament and oftime skill shortage of the Argentinean winch man. There was no evidence to suggest the hatching of dramatic events. Everyday sameness was the order of the day, even now looking back with hindsight; no defining moments or revealing clues missed.

The news that Jane, her mother and Christina were leaving the ship was hard for me to accept. They were scheduled to complete a round voyage. The plan was that a two to three weeks stay in Argentina would allow the Anderson family and Christina to stay with relatives in Rosario and then re-join the ship.

I watched the remaining stevedores walking up the gangway. They came to work in suits. Changing to working clothes and back again before returning home.

Strenuous labour, but better paid than working on an estancia in the Pampas, as Tom pointed out. Their attitude toward dress in contrast to British dockers who would come and go in work clothes. The Argentinean stevedores kept going, apart from a short break, but no siestas. There was plenty of competition, with others waiting to take their place.

A little vino during the midday break, led to tongues loosening. 'You like senoritas, si?' One stevedore might ask. The question led into describing attributes of the Argentinean female. That their daughters would make good wives. Look after of their husbands, but good mothers and home makers. Although their heroine Eva Peron did much to promote women's enfranchisement, this work force believed that women were still like chattels. Whenever the stevedores spoke to us Tom saw it as a distraction technique, intended to occupy our attention while others in the group stole cargo.

Not for the first time that day Tom came on deck shouting

'Que pasa, que pasa,'—basically—'what's going on here, you maniacs on the winches?' As a crate crashed on to the deck. The winch man having miscalculated distance, weight or both. He did not continue in Spanish, making them believe he only grasped a few phrases, not giving away the fact that he spoke the lingo as a native born Argentinean. Tom possessed an air of authority, that I lacked, then. It was Monday, 21st December, 1962, a hot Summer's day, with heat building up. The air below deck was putrid, but we were on deck patrol. All five holds were discharging cargo, when I noticed Captain and Mrs Anderson, Jane and Christina about to disembark.

We got a wave from Jane and Christina as they stepped from the gangway. This effectively left Mr Thompson, the First Mate in charge, as Captain. Just then, dressed in white boiler suit, he came down the companionway, followed by a tally clerk carrying a clipboard. 'Whisky's being unloaded from the special cargo locker, follow me, you two,' he said, entering the masthead locker. We followed. A draft of warm air circulating through the manhole, smelt of garlic but, not sufficiently to obliterate the rank stench of urine in the mast house.

I followed Tom down the ladder, turning to grasp the hooped metal handholds as my feet sought ladder rungs. The special cargo locker was situated at the forward end of the 'tween deck. A padlock secured the locking bars across the double doors. A stevedore's head appeared above the lower hold ladder as we lifted the bars to open the locker. 'Buena tarde senor chief,' he called out, smilingly, but respectful. The Mate lifted an arm in acknowledgement, as we swung back the steel plated doors, securing them with hooks. A deep, rich aroma of whisky came from two rows of blending barrels. These sat in wooden cradles. Hundreds of boxes of whisky, gin, brandy and Drambuie, stowed behind. Tom was directed to stand near the entrance.

I was given the clipboard to tally quantities. There was a three inch metal lip below the open doors. This was part of the reason for the cargo watch. A barrel could be made to smash on to the lip, as it swung outward, held by rope slings. The resulting flow of spirit, then caught in mugs. Apart from interrupting this manoeuvre, there were the cargo hooks, used to grab and lever out tightly packed boxes. Their alternative use was to rip open the box and remove its contents. Once the barrels were safely removed things quietened down. There were three tally counts for the boxes of spirits. Mine, the tally clerk on deck and one in the lorry. We agreed on the box numbers, but as Tom mentioned, that did not guarantee that all held bottles.

The banging on the cabin door must have woken me, but the first words I heard after turning in that evening were. 'Wake up Mike.' It was Tom , knocking the door. It didn't seem like morning, as I pulled back the covers. I switched on the main light by the door. Being woken in the middle of the night, in sleep drugged state, the bright light made me blink. Rubbing my eyes, I glanced at my watch on the tray, by the bunk. Ten past two. I twisted the Yale door catch.

'What the heck's going on Tom, it's the middle of the night.' 'We've got to launch the motorised lifeboat on this side of the ship. They've been prevented from going to the airport. They can't get back on board, the swing bridges have been opened.' There was anxiety in his voice as he went to pull back the porthole curtain, in an attempt to make me more awake. He sat on the day bed, but was on his feet again.

'Look Mike, The Second Engineer's back on board. He was the last person to cross the bridge on to the dock before it was swung open. A taxi arrived on the other side. He heard the driver ordering the passengers out. He was shouting, 'Dios mio, dios mio' and 'guerre civil.' He continued shouting out 'guerre civil' as he put the luggage on the ground.

'Guerre civil, meaning?' I asked, not in sufficient functioning state to interpret meaning—'I got it that he was swearing,' I said. Tom grasped the side of the bunk, shaking his right hand at me to emphasis urgency. 'Sharpen up Mike. There's a civil war starting. Sec says everyone's fled from the streets and shops in town. Tanks are parked outside government buildings with swarms of camouflaged soldiers, doubling through streets. They're trapped on the other side of the bridge. The 'Old Man's said The lifeboat's to be launched. It's the only way they can be rescued. The radio's playing military music and earlier they announced that the rebels have control of the city.'

# Chapter 41

# Rescue by Lifeboat

'When you say the lifeboat's being launched, who else is involved?' I asked. I started putting on my work clothes, my arms and legs only just getting used to the idea of mobility. 'The Mate said when he woke me that since I obtained a Lifeboat certificate I was qualified to take charge with you as bowman and Bill Mackay to operate the engine.' 'What about the dock police, the Marineros?' 'They've scarpered , they're on the regime's side and don't want to be caught by the rebels. With the Fourth's manning the engine, there'll be three of us. The bridge is no distance from here, with ladders on both sides. We just have to motor over and get them aboard, take them to the wall on the other side and return. The Mate's taking a group ashore to meet them. That's if no one intercepts us on the way over.'

'It's true what they say Mike about the Captain having a revolver for emergencies. Merchant ships were purported to have a strait jacket, hand cuffs and a revolver, stored in the Captain's cabin. The Mate's wearing an army canvas type belt, with a revolver in the holster,' continued Tom 'You said the Marineros have left. Is it safe out there?' 'That's what we'll find out. We'd best dress in dark clothing, not anything white.' 'You're making it sound like a commando raid, not a lifeboat rescue,' I said.

The boat deck was the next deck up. Captain Anderson must have done some pretty quick thinking. The starboard lifeboat had an engine and the ship was portside to the jetty. The other boat was kitted out with oars and a sail, which would have made it difficult to manoeuvre in the dock area. I followed Tom to the Boat deck.

179

'Ready for a bit of boating boys?' asked Angelo, who was standing at one end of the boat and the Bosun the other. The cover was lying by the funnel. There was a whirring sound as the Bosun lifted the white release lever. The davits moved out lowering the boat to deck level. The Fourth Engineer arrived in his white overalls—so much for Tom's dark disguise. 'This is something I never want to do for real,' he said, stepping into the boat, that was rocking from being lowered to the ship's side. 'Now comes the acid test.' He opened the engine housing to switch on the fuel. After several swings of the starting handle there was a cough and splutter, followed by a burst of smoke from the stern as fumes poured out. 'You know where you're going?' questioned the Bosun. 'You've got torches?' 'Yes and yes,' said Tom, producing a torch from his donkey jacket. 'The bridge is around the next quay by the Japanese freighter. The one with heavy lift gear.'

'You've got it lad. We'll lower you down. When you come back, tie up alongside—couple of the boys will see to the boat. You got that.' 'Yes, bosun,' got it,' said Tom. It was a jerky ride to the water, with a stopping and starting as the Bosun tried to keep control of the descent. The final ten feet seemed faster than the earlier part as we splashed into the water. The racing engine, slowed as cooling water from the dock entered the system. I released the pulley and hook from the for'ard davit—Tom the after one. 'Slow Ahead Fourth,' ordered Tom.

'Never thought I'd be taking orders from an apprentice,' said Bill as he pushed the lever forward to start the prop shaft turning. It was dark save for the masthead lights that shone from ships in the adjacent dock. Tom said the Mate told him to head for the forward mast of the Japanese freighter ahead, to clear the nearby jetty. In less than ten minutes we were clear of our dock and entering the next. We saw torch flashes from the bridge we needed to get to. 'Thank goodness for that,' said Tom. 'Slow it a bit Bill. I don't want to go in too fast.' The fast pop of the engine exhaust died to a pedestrian pace. 'Here Mike get an oar out, in case we need to fend off.' I pulled an oar out from the bottom of the boat and stood holding it up like a boarding hook. The gap left by the opened swing bridge must have been about fifty feet. We sort of crunched alongside, at the point where Captain Anderson, family and Christina were trapped above, next to the metal ladder. 'What took you so long,' Captain Anderson, exclaimed from the top of the ladder. But I saw relief on Mrs Anderson, Jane and Christina's faces. A whistle came from the other side. The Mate, Mr Thomson was holding up a coil of rope, shining a torch on it. 'Good old Bert. 'I overheard Captain Anderson saying to Mrs Anderson and then to Jane and Christina, 'You two girls can go first we'll stay to lower the luggage. On second thoughts,' he knelt and in a raised voice said, 'Take my daughter and Nurse Wilkins across and bring back the rope the Mate has. One of you two lads can come up here then and assist with lowering the luggage. Okay with that?' Tom raised his head and cupped his hands over his mouth before calling out 'Yes, sir.'

We watched as first Christina and then Jane stepped backwards on to the vertical ladder. I noticed Tom averting his eyes, short skirts not protecting their modesty. Most probably because Christina, would have torn him off a strip for peeping. Bill and me grabbed an arm as they stepped from the ladder to the boat. I then went to the bow to ease the boat away from the wall with the oar as Tom pushed the tiller right across before calling out Slow Ahead.

'You two all right?' asked Bill. 'Glad to see you and the boat,' replied Jane. 'The taxi driver just wanted to get home after we saw truckloads of soldiers in Buenos Aires.' Christina and Jane sat opposite each other just forward of the engine. We were fast heading for the concrete walling on the other side with the tiller amidships. 'You need to shut the engine Tom,

181

probably need to go astern we're going plenty fast enough,' I said turning and shouting back. 'Stop the engine Bill. 'The engine quietened and I reached out from the bow with the oar to hook on to a chain by the ladder. Tom managed to turn the bow away from the wall while going astern. I held on at the bow and Tom the stern. It was darker that side of the bridge.

'It's all right for you Tom Blake we're not dressed for climbing rusty ladders,' said Christina. Tom attempted to be helpful by shining the torch to where she was, about three rungs up. 'You can switch that off for a start, she said. 'I don't want to be the maid in what the butler saw, thank you.' The light went out. Jane, brushed the hair from her face and said, 'Don't think the lady would have said that to the knight, when rescued do you Mike?' 'Probably not,' I replied. Neither Christina nor Tom heard this comment. I was overjoyed that Jane was safe and re-joining the ship, even if Tom didn't meet the knight in shining armour profile for Christina.

'Mind yourselves,' the Mate called out after both Jane and Christina were safely disembarked. The coiled rope smacked on to the engine housing, narrowly missing the Fourth 'Mike you'll need that,' shouted Tom above the engine's noise. It became apparent that it was my task to shin up the ladder to help Captain Anderson lower the luggage into the boat. I reached back from the bow, picked the rope up and slung it over my shoulders. 'Push the bow out,' said Tom. I held the blade end of the oar to lever away from the wall. 'And what have you done to upset Nurse Christina,' I heard Bill asking Tom. 'Nothing.' 'You're not her best friend, that's obvious.' Tom wasn't going to admit he'd led Christina on in not mentioning Rosa. Tom didn't encourage further conversation, but concentrated with the task in hand.

'Give us slow ahead Bill.' We repeated the manoeuvre to get back to the other side. I counted thirty rungs to the top of the ladder. Captain Anderson held a hand out to help me on to the metal bridge, then directed me in securing the rope to the cases. 'Round turn and two half hitches. A clove hitch is all right for lowering buckets. Wrap the rope tightly around that case,' he said as I started tying the largest one. 'It'll be the one with the most valuables in—it belongs to Mrs Anderson.' 'Don't take any notice Mike, you're managing very well,' she said, smiling at me. It was the first time I'd witnessed this husband and wife relationship between them, realizing that they were like any other married couple.

Why would a Captain of a ship have any more clout than the next married man? A ship's Captain shared the lot of ordinary mortals when a husband. Being kept in check by Mrs Anderson was transformational in my appreciation of how the Captain's authority was not as absolute as it might appear. Mrs Anderson thanked us for coming to the rescue, once they were on board the boat. 'What's the plan for the boat?' asked Captain Anderson. The Bosun and some of the crew are going to see to it after we're alongside. 'In that case the luggage can stay where it is.' 'Not the handbags,' interjected Mrs Anderson. 'Except for the handbags,' continued the Captain. After the Captain and Mrs Anderson were disembarked I climbed the ladder and lowered the rope down. Tom tied each handbag individually while I held out my arm to feed the rope through at the top of the ladder avoiding any knocks against the quay wall, assisted by Jane and Christina. Such are the priorities that arise when civil war breaks out in a foreign country.

# Chapter 42

# Jane and Christina Back On Board

The tall black bow of Albany Princess made the boat seem very small as we returned. I spotted three figures on the quay. 'Throttle back,' said Tom to the Fourth just as the Bosun shouted 'Watch yourselves.' He swung the monkey's fist, before letting go the line. It went over the lifeboat, the weighted ball splashed into the water 'You can switch that engine off now, and lash the line round the thwart. We'll pull you alongside. We won't want—then to be needing a new lifeboat.'

Tom looked a bit put out. The Bosun casting aspersions on his boat handling skills. It was a wise move, since beneath the dock were concrete pillars. The rubber fenders didn't extend to water level. It also meant the boat could be pulled alongside next to the ladder. The Bosun was swaying, not overly sober, but did understand small boats, having started working life as a fisherman. Tom grabbed a metal hook in the pillar at the stern, while the line held the bow in. 'Be leaving the luggage now in the boat. The lads will see to it once we've hoisted it up to the davits,' called down the Bosun. It made sense, for ease of luggage removal, the boat being stowed on the passenger and Captain's deck.

Two deckhands, more nimble than us, virtually ran backwards down the ladder and boarded. 'You're okay Fourth—I test ran this boat in Liverpool. That's if you want to leave,' the first one said. 'You bet, we'll leave it in your capable hands.' We followed Bill into the Engineer's Mess and made coffee, taking it with us to the smoke room. The clock was near to seven. It must have taken three hours, but adrenaline flow staved off any feeling of tiredness.

I heard footsteps along the corridor. 'They're in the Smoke Room,' Bill called out from the Mess. Mr Thompson entered shortly afterwards. 'Good bit of seamanship and you didn't damage the boat, according to the Bosun,' he said. Tom looked pleased at this. 'There's unlikely to be any cargo working, the Old Man's been informed that the army are meeting in the dock. Chips though is re-caulking the passenger deck you can help him after you've breakfasted,' the Mate said in a matter of fact sort of way.

The bar room shutter rattled up. 'Good morning Mr Chief, sir.' It was Wann. 'Will there—Mr Chief be extra persons for breakfast meal?' 'Yes four more Wann, you can inform the Chief Cook'. 'It is good to have the three ladies back on board, after holiday.' 'Yes, Wann, but it wasn't a holiday,' said the Mate. At this point Jane and Christina walked into the Smoke Room. 'No it wasn't a holiday Wann,' said Jane. 'We did see your girlfriend though,' continued Christina seeking to mix things. 'What girlfriend?—Wann happy bachelor.'

'Senorita Eva. In an army truck wearing a colonel's uniform,' said Jane. 'That senorita no girlfriend for Wann. She no like me. She very unfriendly lady.' He showed disdain by flicking his serving cloth on the bar, as if swotting a fly. 'But you are all right Miss Jane? When they captured that bad lady I was wanting to stab her with knife, but Chief Cook no let me have knife. Very bad, no like. Very good when make free by sea frogmen.' This was Wann's interpretation of the boarding by Lieutenant Payne and the commandos. 'I'm all right Wann and it's probably just as well you didn't attack her. She's very high ranking, and they've taken over the city.'

'I understand Miss Taylor, from your father that for diplomatic reasons they were released, in Montevideo, to return to Argentina. Everything's very fluid and it's anyone's guess who will end up in control,' said the Mate. Wann, smiled across to where we were before pulling the bar shutter closed. 'They're part of the rebel army faction, but if they control Buenos Aires and may take over the Presidential Pink Palace. There's no telling who will end up with political control—it could even be Eva and her sidekick. It's probably lucky nothing happened to them, for our sakes.'

He placed his hand on the top of the chair Jane was sitting in before continuing. 'Your father told me that you're happy to continue working, Miss Taylor. Perhaps after midday, when you've rested you can assist these two renegades,' he said pointing at us two. 'They're working on the re-caulking of the bridge deck, later today, assisting Chippy. They'll need a steady hand later to pour pitch into the planks. Chippy said you missed out last time?' 'Yes,' said Jane, 'I love the tarry smell of melting pitch. I wanted to have a go last time.' Tom looked at me quizzically, as if to say, 'What's that got to do with anything?' Imaginative appreciation of such things not really being on Tom's radar. The recent fall out with Christina, perhaps reduced his empathy with what he saw as trivial, inconsequential female perceptions.

'And Nurse Wilkins.' Mr Thompson turned to Christina now sat opposite us. 'You're not redundant with Miss Devlin and her brother ashore. Hopefully, safe and not in the hands of some military faction. Mrs Anderson has scraped her leg climbing a ladder. I found a dressing, perhaps you can cast your professional eye over it. Also an afternoon surgery for the crew would be appreciated. Is that possible?' 'Yes, that's fine,' said Christina. 'We're relieved to be back aboard, aren't we Jane?' Both smiled rather flatteringly, I thought, at the Mate. But then Mr Thompson wasn't going to let the prospects of a civil war interfere with his work schedule for the day.

# Chapter 43

# War Confirmation

The news during breakfast on Sunday in the saloon was not good. 'How do you know that?' Sparks, asked Charlie. He was recovered from his ordeal as a hostage, and was two chairs down from where I was sitting. 'I was on deck at seven when the agent boarded. He told Mr Thompson that cargo unloading was postponed because the army plans to meet in the docks today. The President's holed up in his palace surrounded by tanks and truck loads of rebel soldiers. The army loyal to him is meeting in Dock Sud, but they don't want to fight, the agent said.

'Was that supposed to reassure us?' asked Sparks. I didn't hear the reply, because Tom arrived followed by Jane and Christina. 'The Chief's just said we can have the day off,' he said, pulling back the chair opposite. I told Tom about the conversation I'd just overheard. 'That's probably why he's also said we're to stay inside and only go out at dusk to take the flags down. He doesn't want us shot,' said Tom, I thought rather unconvincingly.

'Rice Crispies Miss Jane? Orange juice for you Miss Christina?' Asked Wann after clearing away the plates from where Charlie and Sparks were sitting. Wann accustomed to this order from Jane and Christina. 'Don't we have a choice asked Christina?' 'But of course. I not take Miss Christina for granted,' 'Who would ever dare do that?' said Tom under his breath. 'I'll have Corn Flakes then Wann, please.' 'I'm fine with Rice Crispies.' added Jane. 'Mr Tom is it for you usual—sunny side up egg, sausage, bacon, toast and coffee. Or perhaps you also try corn flakes?' Wann was treading on dangerous ground knowing the fall out between Tom and Christina. 'I don't want corn flakes Wann. No I'll stick with the usual.' 'Muy bueno, uno momento, Senor Tom y senoritas.' The Spanish thrown in by Wann possibly to impress or humour Tom—it could have been either.

There was a distant crackling sound. Mr Thompson walked into the saloon followed by the shipping agent. 'That noise like Chinese fire crackers,' said Wann on his way back to the dumb waiter to fetch the cereals. The crackling was followed by a deeper rumble. 'Don't want to alarm anyone,' said Mr Thompson, 'but the rebels are firing at buildings around Buenos Aires. Isn't that right senor Gomez?' 'Si ,si, I'm 'fraid it is so Chief Officer. Not fire crackers they're real guns firing.' Until the gunfire everything seemed normal tied up alongside the dock. The ship was quiet, save for the hum of the generator.

Normally the jarring and crashing of derricks lifting with wires on crates might have drowned out gunfire from the City. The derricks were hoisted ready, but the tarpaulins and locking bars were still in place over the holds. The newly painted deck around the holds a glistening red. Unsullied by the detritus of broken timber; the white dust from split clay bags and hastily stubbed out cigarette ends around mast houses. The ship miniaturised would have looked impressive in a glass display case. The accommodation was red leaded and yet to be painted with white gloss, but I considered that would give authenticity for a working ship.

My mind diverted from the moment inexplicably. An antidote, perhaps to the ongoing seriousness of the situation. We left Jane and Christina to the tender mercies of Wann and were returning to our cabins when the top and bottom lugs of the engine room door moved. It swung open and Bill stepped into the corridor, after vigorously wiping his shoes on the mat between the double doors.

'We're wanting to do work on the cooling pipes and he's needing us to be on Stand By. Stand By—to go where?' he

188

demanded. Tom understood the situation better than me and gave an explanation.

'Captain Anderson might want to leave. Take the ship back to sea.' 'What without tugs?' 'It can be done,' said Tom. 'And we have to stand around like spare parts until he makes up his mind?' Bill continued. 'Yes, until he knows what's happening. Tanks are firing near to Buenos Aires city centre.' I realized that Bill wouldn't have heard the gun fire down in the engine room. It was December and hot outside, never mind down the engine room. Probably frustrating, having to keep the engine on Stand By, unable to do essential maintenance.

Apart from hearing the explosions we had nothing else to tell Bill. Chris, the Second Steward came around with letters that the agent brought on board. We later drifted into the Engineers Mess for coffee. Bill was showing Charlie a photo of his baby daughter. I still expected Leckie to walk in. There was empathy in the shared sense of loss, but there was no talk of the hijack today. The way Pepe and Eva were released and allowed to return to Argentina from Uruguay after shooting Leckie. The British Foreign Office's attempt to avoid a diplomatic incident over riding his killing.

The talk was about babies for the moment. 'It is the way they're perfectly formed. It's just amazing when they're so small,' said Charlie. The conversation a diversion from the tension and also, in particular, the delight that Bill had in showing everyone the picture of his baby daughter.

Late that afternoon Tom barged into my cabin. 'Come and listen to this on the radio,' he said. The station's martial music interposed with rapid speech, filtered in from his cabin. 'You'll have to translate,' I said, as I stood next to the transistor on Tom's desk. It was a woman speaking like a rapid fire machine gun. 'She's saying Argentina has a new leader, who is going to restore calm to this great country. General Romera leader of the army in Buenos Aires has appealed for calm. The fighting is finished and he will be General and President for all the peoples of Argentina, until a new President is elected. The streets are safe. The whole of the military recognizes General Romera as leader and President. Viva Presidente General Romera. Shortly he will speak personally to all Argentineans on this station. Vive El General.' Martial Music followed.

'What does that mean? Is it true?' I asked Tom. 'That the fighting's over.' 'Yes, I've been following the reports. General Romera is leader of the rebel faction, but he is in control of Buenos Aires and the army loyal to the President has recognized him as supreme commander. The President has resigned. I must go and tell the Mate.' I wondered if Mrs Anderson heard the broadcast. I couldn't imagine anyone else on board following the radio broadcast the way Tom was able to. 'What does that mean for us,' I asked Tom before he charged off. 'We'll most likely be cargo watching tomorrow.'

Tomorrow being Monday. Tom was right. I'd never seen the stevedores work at such a pace. Tom reverted to shouting at them in Spanish, breaking his anonymity of being only able to speak English. We left just over a week later on the Tuesday, according to my journal, and escaped from the civil and military strife in Buenos Aires to the calmer atmosphere of Rosario. Tall grain silos and warehouses near to the river bank with the occasional ship moored alongside on the town side of the river.

# Chapter 44

# Last Day On Board

Jane, her mother and Christina came back on board. The civil war having interrupted their departure in Buenos Aires. They went for a few days to stay with Jane's granny and to meet Jane's Aunt Rayen and two uncles, but were back on board for a day before we left Rosario. It was a goodbye visit, although I didn't know it at the time. Mr Thomson arranged for the lifeboat to be tested. The one not used in the rescue, but with only sail and oars. It was lowered and brought around to steps leading to the river's edge. Wann prepared sandwiches. We took cans of Coke and Seven Up from the fridge, I remember.

Mr Thompson gave instructions from the riverside after we boarded. 'There's a staging post a little way upstream. You're supposed to be testing the sails, but if you chance to go ashore don't let the boat out of your sight,' he said to Tom. We moved away from the riverbank, with Tom and me rowing and Jane steering. 'We're only here for the day,' she said. 'The British embassy found out Pepe and Eva were members of the rebel army faction, which is now the government. The ship may be at risk. We're being flown back to the UK straight away.'

They were obviously not overly worried about the crew or ship just Jane, Christina and Mrs Anderson, it appeared. Tom considered himself an expert at handling boats. The lifeboat with sails was on the river side of the ship, enabling it to be launched. On board there was still an element of relief. Everyday experiences take on a new poignancy after life threatening events. Jane and Christina decided they wanted to have a go at rowing. 'That's a bit risky,' said Tom,—'bringing the camera,' as I produced it from a canvas grip, that contained the cans of drink and sandwiches. I was at the tiller while Jane and Christina were "catching crabs," trying to row together. Just as I snapped the picture Tom placed both hands over his eyes from where he was standing in the bow. 'Risky, it is if—you're in the picture,' said Christina turning towards Tom. 'You didn't have to do that Tom,' I said. 'Do what?' asked Jane. 'Put your hands over your eyes, and open your mouth in horror just as I took the photo,' 'I bet you were just as hopeless at rowing the first time you tried,' said Christina. 'Take no notice Jane.' Whatever serious affection Christina shared with Tom earlier back in the UK now seemed to have become more one of tolerance bordering on irritation. The hijack, if anything drew Jane and Christina closer. It was no use denying, it was a bitter sweet experience for me. Jane and Christina were only on board for the day. It was sensible to accept that it was no good revealing my feelings towards her. I, that individual walking the earth, made captive to the way she smiled, talked, walked dressed. Affirming with positives all she found interesting. One friendly smile, lighting up and making happy every cell in my body. The madness of this state. I might have been Aladdin, but not with his confidence. A junior apprentice falling for the Captain's daughter. What chance did I have? It was Eva, with her evil intent that actually informed me as to the degree of my real feelings for Jane. Those feelings then in Jane's presence, made me feel generous toward Tom, as he once again went too far in annoying the three of us.

This was why the news that the three women were leaving the ship hit me badly. It was a sad, sad, situation, like the song informs. 'Might see them at the Electric Hall, said Tom, after arriving back, but he wasn't that bothered. There was one more run to South America and then we split up. Tom went ashore to study for his Second Mate's certificate. I transferred to another ship.

# Epilogue

Ocean Melody Approaches Montevideo
November 12th, 1968

I advanced the Giro course heading by one degree. The position from six star sights placed us east of the course line. I estimated that a one degree alteration would bring us back on course by midday when the Sun's altitude at midday was taken. Ocean Melody having then covered a day's run of about 120 miles.

The Port of Liverpool was now a distant memory. We were in the Southern Hemisphere, heading for Montevideo. A name that conjured up memories of the hijack in 1962. The door into the chart room clicked open. 'That's good you've managed to get a star sight.' Dave, the First Mate called out before entering the Wheel House. 'Anything about?' he asked. 'Occasional north bound traffic, nothing much. We're gradually being overhauled by an Italian liner on the port side, but well clear of us. The course is now 186 not 185.'

'Yes, I can see by your star sight we've moved off course. Never can tell what the ocean's about, but that should get us back. One eight six it is then,' he said, checking the compass repeater, before we went on to the bridge to get a look at the liner. 'Left a torch on your desk Mike with the Montevideo cargo listings. Appreciate your taking a look down the holds before you take over the watch midday. Just check I've only blue tagged the cargo due to go ashore in Montevideo and no other. Another experienced pair of eyes giving it a once over wouldn't go amiss,' said Dave. 'The exercise will do me good. I need to get familiar again with the layout on deck and down the holds.' 'All right you'd best get below and get some sleep, while we're not jumping about on Atlantic rollers.'

Three days later and we swapped the ocean blue sea for the muddy pond colour of the River Plate Estuary, preparing to dock at Montevideo. I remembered the visit to the mission after the hijack leading to the discovery that Christina, Jane and her mother were leaving the ship and flying back to the UK. Ocean Melody stopped for a day and then five days in Buenos having discharged the final three thousand tons of cargo, before going up river to Rosario for grain.

The years immediately following my apprenticeship I was somehow destined to work on ship's trading away from Argentina. I knew that memories of that day spent with Jane and Christina aboard the lifeboat would dominate my thoughts as we tied up alongside the granary quay in Rosario. The last time the four of us were together. There was no reason we should have kept in touch. After working aboard ten or more ships other memories crowded into the storage bank of—life at sea experience. The Albany Princess was my first ship and it was hijacked. Reuters reported the incident in a small column. 'Royal Navy boards Motor Vessel Albany Princess before midnight GMT December 20th due to disturbance from passengers returning to Buenos Aires'.

It was reported as a disturbance. It was a lesson in not believing what you read in the press. Pepe and Eva, taking over the ship, holding Jane and the Radio Officer hostage. Threatening to shoot anyone who did not do exactly as they demanded—that went unreported—and then leading to Leckie dying from gunshot wounds. That they and their group of so called freedom fighters joined the rebel army in Buenos Aires, on release in Montevideo, and assisted in overthrowing the existing government. None of that came out, but there were no satellites to give instant news to the wider world.

Never believe what you read in the press from so called "official sources." Those of us spat at by the military in Argentina, affirmed resentment at the Falklands not being Argentinean—we knew about the level of hostility, but did the British Government choose to pretend it never existed?

On arriving at Rosario on board Ocean Melody when the warp on the winch crunched and pulled the stern closer to the jetty it could have been six years ago. The ramshackle dock building, rusting roofs of the warehouses remembered from those days, but perhaps a little more neglected.

The Argentinean ship loading grain on the jetty across from us, possibly one that was trading around the coast when I was aboard the Albany Princess. The boiler suit I put on over the white tropical uniform was not the clean white associated with a cargo liner, as I prepared for working on deck. A spattering of black oil marks remained on the legs, stained in from oil blowing out of a sighting cap as we topped off loading in Nigeria. There was an uprising and talk of tribal war.

Rosario, by contrast seemed sleepy and unthreatening. I understood why officers opted to stay on this run, with a two or three week stay on the coast. First discharging and then getting together an assorted cargo from Rosario, Bahia Blanca, Buenos Aires and then a short stop at Montevideo before the three week passage back to the UK. On this run it was not so much a girlfriend in every port, but could be a second partner, who waited for the return of the ship.

Captain Bellamy partnered a vivacious, volatile dark skinned Latin woman, who came aboard when we docked. They were now in Mar del Plato while Dave Green the Mate took charge There was a son by this relationship, although no children by his wife back in Liverpool Dave Green informed me. As I stepped out on to the gangway accommodation I wondered whether she knew that there was a possibility the ship might no longer dock in Buenos Aires. Aged twenty three I didn't have complicated relationships.

A sister younger by two years introduced me to her girlfriends, which did lead to one or two being asked out. I remembered the Fifth Engineer aboard the Albany Princess who moved from girl friend to girlfriend. Quite happy to move on to a replacement model, so to speak, waiting in a foreign port. Did he get caught or is he now just older and have the women become tired of waiting?

There was always the demanding mistress—the sea and an attention seeking ship. In this case—Steam Ship Ocean Melody.

'I won't be able to show them around or talk about the ship,' I heard the Mate say to the Chief Steward as they came out and stopped by the gangway. 'Just the man,' said Dave Green as he saw me. 'For what?' I asked. 'To explain to a group of students what happens on board a ship.' 'That shouldn't take long. The Third Mate might relate to them, better than me,' I said, not very keen on the idea 'No, there might be some complex questions, needing specialist answers. The attempt at flattery didn't overwhelm me at the time, I remember.

'It's a bit of a public relations exercise, on the company's part,' continued Dave. 'Apparently the teacher's family have past connection with the company. It's a bit much to expect the Third to cope. They're due at two. At four you can park them in the smoke room. The Chief Steward will give them fizzy drinks and biscuits.' 'I knew I wouldn't be getting away without being a contributor,' said the Chief.

'You Know the drill. They'll want a look in the engine room, which means getting the go ahead from the Chief Engineer first. That shouldn't be a problem. Take the junior apprentice with you. He's closer in age to any of us crusty seafarers—Don't take them on to the main deck. The wheelhouse and bridge are as safe a vantage point, as any to describe what's going on and answer questions.' 'You haven't totally sold the idea to me, but it looks like I've been volunteered, if that's the right expression,' I said.

'I'm sure you'll be able to hold their attention with some daring exploits. That time you helped foil a hijack, on board Albany Princess. No need to mention the Falklands being

196

involved. You could say it was piracy. That there was gold bullion on board. Give them something to write about.' 'I suppose it's convenient that nothing got out about what really happened,' I said, 'from the company's point of view and relations with Argentina.' 'That's what trade relations are about. Keeping foreign nationals sweet, so they go on buying what Britain makes.'

'The whisky and spirits, you mean,' I said. 'There's not much in the way of manufactured goods. There's stiff competition from the Americans, Japanese and Germans.' 'That's all fixed, then I can leave it in your capable hands. Two o'clock, remember. Should be able to get lunch,' and with that Dave went into the accommodation. After lunch I went up to the Boat Deck, which meant being clear from the bustle around the gangway. There was a peep from a Collectivo bus.

These are private single decker Mercedes buses owned by the driver. The one now parked inside the dock gates not being allowed to go any further. I was intrigued, because the bus brought back memories. The coloured streamers attached to the wing mirrors. The flags along the inside of the windscreen. Lucky charms suspended to the side of the driver. Most likely a framed picture of the driver's family attached to the dashboard. Each driver personalized the cab to make it individual to him.

The sight of this vehicle, more a miniature coach than bus, brought back memories of the journeys made five years ago when ashore. The clicking of levers released the coins in change from the gleaming chrome canister at the side of the driver. The garlic and vino on the breath of passengers mixed with individual Latin American cigarette aroma.

I was lost in this remembered world when the Fourth Engineer said, 'Good luck with the guided tour then, there looks to be a bus load of them.' 'Really,' I said not having registered the connection, lost in my memories. 'They're on that

197

bus, can't you see?' We were stood overlooking the gangway. The Fourth in a boiler suit on deck chain smoking a cigarette. Away from the grain dust below. Sure enough, several teenagers in jeans and T shirts had left the bus. 'You're right,' I said, 'wish me luck.' I lost sight of them as I went through the accommodation to the boarding deck below. I opened the door on to that deck and heard the rattle of the aluminium gangway as they came aboard. I stood back against the bulkhead. They poured on to the deck. There must have been about twenty, thirteen to fourteen year olds. I looked for an adult male teacher, but could not see one.

Further along the corridor the Chief Steward was talking to a woman in a scarf sunglasses and a long white coat with her head turned away from me. I realized that she must be the teacher in charge of the party. They were having difficulty hearing each other above the babble of the students. The teacher turned and shouted 'Silencio.' The voice whipped a surge of love and affection through my body transcending time itself.

I realized it was Jane. She turned away, but back again, having spotted me. She removed her sunglasses, but did not wave. The Second Steward started talking to the Chief and she walked across to where I was by the gangway. 'Hello Mike. remember me?' As if the possibility of forgetting her was ever going to happen. 'Of course I do,' I replied. 'I knew it would be dusty. I'm in work clothes,' she said as if it made any difference to me how she was dressed when I was so thrilled at seeing her again. 'You look surprised or is there something the matter?' 'Of course not, I mean, only that—what are you doing here?' There was an element of deja vue about this I realized later. 'Am I not allowed on board then?' she said. 'Do I need a pass?' 'No it's not that I was expecting a male teacher and I never knew you lived here. I believed you returned to the UK.' I didn't let on Tom told me the Anderson family had moved to Argentina.

198

'It didn't turn out as expected. I stayed with my grandmother. Christina met my cousin and hey presto they got married, not straightaway. My mother flew home to sell the house. I trained as an English teacher and I'm a teacher and live on the estancia. Uno momento—silencio!' She broke away to take charge of her group. I'd prepared to meet a man and not Jane. I remember thinking she looked shorter, but maybe I was taller.

In the six intervening years it was possible I could have grown. The Chief Steward came across from by the gangway to talk to Jane. 'This is Second Officer Peters. Mr Green the Chief Officer is unable to show you around. At four o'clock there will be refreshments in the dining saloon.' 'That's perfectly all right Chief Steward I'm sure the Second officer will be just as knowledgeable—muchas gracius.' Jane decided to play along with pretending we did not know each other.

'It is very good of you Second Officer to spare time for this—from your very important duties, she smiled. I reached out to shake her slim hand which disappeared into the palm of mine. I was looking again into those blue green eyes, and smiling face trying to contain itself from breaking into laughter at the deception of already knowing one another. 'I'll leave you in the Second Mate's capable hands,' said the Chief Steward, who went back into the accommodation followed by Pete the Second Steward. The apprentice was standing by my side.

'Go and pay my respects to the Chief Engineer. Ask him if he would like to assist with the guided tour now or later,' I said, wanting to carry on the conversation with Jane. 'Right Sec,' he said and left us. 'This brings back memories,' said Jane. Her students were watching the grain hiss down the pipe into number three hold. I wanted to talk to her.

'This brings back memories,' she said, again, the sudden rush of grain having drowned out the first time she spoke. 'It's a newer looking ship than Albany Princess, but very similar, and now you're Second Mate Mike.' 'And you're a teacher,' I said. 'Where are you allowed to take us?' she asked. I really wanted to talk about how she ended up in Argentina and just generally get up to date, but this was not going to happen while there were twenty or so students milling about.

'Good point. You're not allowed on to the main deck or actually down into the engine room. We're restricted to the accommodation, bridge, boat deck and the Chief Engineer has volunteered to answer questions about the engine room, but only from just inside the engine room doors. Probably the best plan is for you to follow me through into the accommodation and up to the next deck. Yes, also, the Chief has said only five at a time can go into the upper part of the engine room.'

I realized at that moment there was no other place I wanted to be in the world other than with Jane. All turbulence and foreboding thrown out by her presence again in my life. Love takes over, but there are times that you are unaware of its determining presence. I had no doubts about its presence for me at that moment. 'Lead the way, then Mike,' she said, continuing to look and smile at me even when calling out to the students. 'Siguanme.' Meaning follow me. I stepped on to the stairway inside to lead the way and the apprentice all but tumbled down. 'The Chief says he's ready for a question and answer session, but can the teacher act as interpreter?' 'You wouldn't like that job then?' 'Not really Second.' 'Don't look so worried. I was only joking. They lined up along the corridor. The layout was identical to Albany Princess with the toilets, washroom and showers next to the engine room airlocked door. Jane able to direct the students to the facilities.

The Chief Engineer came down the stairs in white tropical uniform the four gold bands epaulettes with the purple lines clearly visible on the shoulders of his shirt. 'Buenas tarde, senorita,' he started by addressing Jane. 'Hello Chief, it's very good of you to give us your time.' The Chief looked pleasantly surprised to be meeting a young woman who spoke English. 'You're not from around here, then?' 'No I'm a refugee from England you could say.' I was about to give the Chief more information, but Jane said, 'The first five are ready, would you like us to follow you? Perhaps Second Officer, you could make sure that only five enter at a time.' She smiled conspiratorially at me, aware that the Chief believed us to be strangers.

He pulled open the latched corners of the door. 'One at time, after me,' he said as he stepped onto the mat in the air locked compartment. 'Jane followed and I supervised each batch as their turn came up. I was glad the Chief helped out by answering questions about the engine room. Jane later said a number of students were studying engineering and the Chief gave them detailed answers. It helped cover the two hours allotted to the tour. Jane chipped in with her experiences of working on board a ship, which meant they got plenty of information. My main input was explaining loading techniques as we looked down from the vantage point of the bridge, but also the navigational aids in the wheel house and chart room.

One or two of them attempted to get a sun azimuth with a sextant using the roof of a ware house as an imaginary horizon. The female students showed more interest in the layout of the accommodation. They were shown the six passenger cabins. At three thirty I took the party down to the dining saloon.

'Do you remember Wann?' Jane asked. 'He was quite disapproving of women having a say about anything.' We sat on a separate table. Extra chairs were positioned around the bulkheads for the students to sit on. They queued up to help themselves from beakers of coke, squash and biscuits. The steward poured tea for a few of them. I remarked to Jane about this. 'Several are from Anglo English families, who will drink tea.' she said. 'What about you,' I asked? 'You're a career woman now then.' 'And you Mike, married with baby Mikes?' 'No, not married, you could say I'm still married to a ship and kept under the thumb of the mistress—the sea.' 'Are you married?—not spoken for are you?' I asked, trying not to sound overly concerned. Jane held out her left hand. 'I take my wedding ring off when I come aboard ships,' she said and looked at me in a serious manner, before smiling. 'Remember at the dance when Tom, asked?' she quickly added. I must have looked worried at this point. She smiled, holding the cup of tea to her mouth, elbows on table. 'No Mike,—I'm not.'

'Christina though would have to answer yes to that question—now, she's married to my cousin.' 'But not you,' I said. 'Not me Mike.' 'You must come and meet Christina and mother and father. Father is up to his ears in muck, as the saying goes. He's a farmer these days.' 'I'd like that, when older, perhaps,' I said. 'I'm not spoken for as you put it, Mike. Would that mean you wouldn't want to see me again? I don't know why I said that.'

'Don't look—on the next table—I'm going to get all sorts of questions from the girl students. Do you think they've spotted that we know each other.' 'No, how could they?' I then realized my arm was stretched across the table, hand open as if it had a mind of its own and was reaching out to take hold of Jane. I moved it back and picked up the cup, but then I was mirror imaging Jane holding the cup in my hands elbows on table. 'They're at that age where all men are discussed as for their merits or otherwise.' 'You say that as if I just represent some broad category and that other than being the opposite sex I hold no interest.' 'I never said that. Mike, I know an Italian style restaurant, where we could meet up with Christina and her husband Carlos—that's if you'd like to—?' It was not quite what I had in my mind, but I said, 'Yes, that sounds like a good idea.' I was encouraged by this and felt my love was being responded to. Jane's smile contained a warmth that stayed with me after she looked away. I was no longer that gawky teenager. The age gap of my twenty three to Jane's twenty nine I felt not a daunting gap for a man and a woman. I just remembered then, Tom saying in the dry dock. 'She's a bit too classy for you Mike.'

END.


### CARGO SHIP Albany Princess: Crew and passenger accommodation listing.

**Deck side:** Captain, First Officer (Chief), Second Mate, Third Mate, Senior Apprentice, Junior Apprentice Bosun , Carpenter, The Radio Officer, Able -Bodied seamen, (ABs), Efficient Deck Hands, (EDHs) and Deck Boy.

**Engineering:** Chief Engineer (Chief), Second Engineer, Third Engineer, Fourth Engineer, Fifth Engineer, Sixth Engineer, Leckie, the Electrician, Boiler room staff (greasers).

**Catering:** Chief Steward (Chief), Second Steward, Dining steward, Chief Cook, Second Cook (Baker). Galley Boy.

**Six passenger berths:** Four passengers- plus two crew members berthed in passenger accommodation.